D0956041

Weekly Reader Children's Book Club presents

MARCO AND
THAT CURIOUS CAT

WEEKLY READER
CHILDREN'S BOOK CLUB

MARCO AND

THAT CURIOUS CAT

by John Foster

Illustrated by

LORENCE F. BJORKLUND

DODD, MEAD & COMPANY
New York

For Dorothy M. Bryan
who rescued Marco from oblivion
and who had much to do with this story

ISBN 0-396-06226-1

Library of Congress Catalog Card Number: 70-123499

Printed in the United States of America
Weekly Reader Children's Book Club Edition
Senior Division

CONTENTS

1. A Letter from the Beyond   1
2. Journey to the Beyond   12
3. Faces in the Fire   27
4. The Footprint   41
5. If Curious Cat Could Talk   50
6. Scouting Expedition   62
7. The Sheriff of Napoleon Parish   75
8. Letters from All Over   89
9. The Curse of the Dantons   104
10. Hurricane Inez   121
11. A Face at the Window   132
12. Lost in Big Green Swamp   143
13. "Get Out of This House!"   157
14. A Knock at the Door   164
15. The Locked Room   175

Some years ago, I explored a lovely old plantation house in New Iberia, Louisiana, on Bayou Teche. It was called "Shadows on the Teche." The National Trust for Historic Preservation had accepted this house and later restored it to the way it had been before the Civil War. Shadows is now open to the public. The house made a deep impression upon me, and when I described the bayou mansion in Marco and That Curious Cat *I was thinking about Shadows, to a large extent. But the events that take place at the Shady Hall [of my story] did not occur at Shadows or anywhere else, except in my imagination. Likewise, the characters in this book are completely fictitious and are not intended to portray anyone who actually lived. I also want to acknowledge the help of James M. Leonard with part of this book, as well as its predecessor,* Marco and the Sleuth Hound.

1

A LETTER FROM THE BEYOND

Down the street, the clock in the belfry of St. Louis Cathedral was carefully chiming three as Marco Fennerty, Junior, came home from delivering his papers. He vaulted off his bike, and wheeled it into the hallway of the apartment house, talking to it softly, complimenting it on a job well done.

The boy's eyes were still dazzled by the afternoon sunlight that flowed like honey through the streets of the French Quarter in New Orleans, and the hallway was dim. But it looked as though there just might be something of interest in the Fennerty mailbox.

Everyday for the past month Marco had been waiting for a certain letter, and every day he had been disappointed. But perhaps today, just possibly. . . . He took the tiny key from his wallet and unlocked the mailbox.

There was a bill from the New Orleans Public Service, addressed to his father. There was a post card to Marco and his father from Mrs. Partridge, the housekeeper, who was visiting relatives in Biloxi. There was a letter for Marco from New Paris, Louisiana (wherever that was) and—yes, yes, indeed—a letter from World Artists Institute, THE letter.

Marco took a deep breath, and tore the long white envelope open. Five long weeks ago he had seen the ad in the paper: "DRAW ME AND WIN A FREE ART COURSE WORTH $1,000." *Me* was the head of a horse.

Ever since he could remember, Marco had been making pictures of all kinds of things, from river boats to tigers, so he had drawn what he and Mrs. Partridge had considered to be an excellent horse's head. He added mountains and clouds in the background for good measure, along with a pair of flying eagles or perhaps hawks, and mailed the drawing to World Artists Institute. He had said nothing to his father because the boy wanted to surprise him. Dad would be so pleased. . . .

Marco let the deep breath out and unfolded the paper. The letter said:

"Dear Friend: Thank you for entering our contest. Of course, you must understand that only one person could win, but we at World Artists Institute feel that your work shows real promise. For only $78.95 we will give you a series of ten art lessons. . . ."

There was more but Marco did not bother to read it.

"*Hmmm,*" he said. "Oh, well," he added, brushing a hand through his shaggy blond hair.

Slowly he climbed the steep stairs to the Fennerty's third-floor apartment. His dejection made him seem smaller than he really was, which was not very big for an eleven-year-old in the first place—except for his ears and dark brown eyes, all of which were quite large indeed.

Outside his door, Marco squared his shoulders and re-marked, "Nuts to them!"

Only when he had entered the apartment did he remember the other letter in his hand. Without much interest, he opened it. It was from his cousin, Lily Delaney, who lived in Baton Rouge, Louisiana.

Shady Hall
New Paris, La.
Sept. 1

Dear Cousin Marco:

I bet you're surprised to be getting a letter from me here 😊 I'm staying with ~~my~~ my great aunt, Hazel Panton, in her big old spooky plantation house. I told her how you and that girl and the sleuth ~~hound~~ hound caught those bad guys and found the Confederate gold, and she wants you to come for a visit 😊

Marco, there's something funny going on here. Aunt Hazel is scared to death but won't admit it 😠 I'm scared too but I admit it 😊

This story from the New Paris Ledger will give you an idea of what I mean.
Please come! You must come!!!

Your "Kissin Cousin"
Miss Lily Delaney

Huh! Marco said to himself. If she thinks I'm going to kiss her, she's got another think coming. But Shady Hall sounded great. He unfolded the newspaper clipping that Lily had enclosed. The headline asked the question:

GHOSTS AT HISTORIC SITE?

"Gungah!" Marco exclaimed. The expression was his own and made no sense at all, but he liked it, and used it whenever it helped the situation.

The story that followed was interesting—up to a point:

Authorities are investigating a series of mysterious happenings at Shady Hall, the stately old mansion on Bayou Terrebonne which has been in the Danton Family since it was built in 1809 or 1810.

Asked to comment upon the mysterious happenings, Miss Hazel Danton, the present occupant, stated: "No comment."

But Sheriff Sam Y. Gross, told the *Ledger* that neighbors had complained of a howling at night and other strange sounds, and mysterious lights coming from the historic site, considered one of the finest examples of a

Creole plantation house still in existence.

Sheriff Gross reported that he would get to the bottom of the mystery.

"I'll get to the bottom of this mystery," he told the *Ledger* in an exclusive interview. "I don't care if there *is* an election coming up!"

The history of Shady Hall—so named because of the mighty oak trees that keep it in gloomy shadow throughout the sunlit hours of the day—includes many tragic and sometimes mysterious deaths, including that of Mr. James "Jim" Danton, Miss Hazel Danton's younger brother.

Mr. Danton passed away in a boating accident on Vermilion Bay on September 4 of last year

(Continued on Page 2)

But there was no more! Good old Lily had forgotten to cut out the rest of the story. Nonetheless, there was enough to go on, although Sheriff Sam Y. Gross—maybe because he was up for re-election—seemed to be making an awful fuss about some sounds and lights. Just the same . . .

Marco looked up New Paris on his road map of Louisiana. He finally found it in the lower right-hand corner of Napoleon Parish, about a hundred miles southwest of New Orleans. It was in the heart of the bayou country, a section of the state which—city boy that he was—he had always considered the boondocks, The Beyond.

Right above New Paris on the map, he saw a large green area marked "Big Green Swamp." Bayou Terrebonne came out of that and flowed into Vermilion Bay about ten miles to the south.

The boy went into his father's room and called Union Station. There was a train leaving for New Paris at 4:17 p.m., arriving at 6:58. Marco glanced at the alarm clock on the night stand. It said 3:22. Not much time—at all. The boy dialed 822-4161.

"Police Department. Sergeant Fennerty speaking."

"Hi, Dad."

"Ah, 'tis Himself," Marco's father crooned in his best Irish brogue. "And what can the likes of me be doin' for the likes of you, bucko?"

"Dad, I got a letter from Lily Delaney. She's staying with her Aunt Hazel Danton in New Paris, and they want me to come for a visit. Can I go?"

"New Paris—where in this wide world may that be now?"

It *had* to be a small place, Marco thought, if his father hadn't heard of it.

"Out in the bayou country, in Napoleon Parish," the boy told him. "Dad, they live in a big spooky house that has a mystery of some kind and maybe a few ghosts!"

"*Ghosts*, is it?" his father exclaimed, still in the brogue.

"Maybe I can solve the mystery," Marco said. "Dad, can I go?"

In the police station he could hear other phones ringing, and the click-clack-click of a typewriter as some officer painfully wrote out a report. As the boy watched the alarm clock, the minute hand jerked downward to five.

"I'll take the matter under advisement," Sergeant Fennerty replied. "How soon do you have to know?"

"Right now. This minute."

"Ho, sits the wind in that quarter!" His father was now a sea captain in some other period of history.

"Dad, there's a train leaving here for New Paris in less than an hour. Dad, please, *can I go*?"

"You have money?"

"Yes."

"What about your paper route?"

"I'll get another kid."

The Irishman was gone, and so was the sea captain. Sergeant Fennerty came on in his usual way, a tough but kindly

New Orleans policeman:

"Okay, Marco, you can go. Send me a wire as soon as you get there, and be careful. AND," he added, "you be back Sunday night at the latest, you hear? School starts Monday."

The boy groaned, "School!"

"That's an order, Son."

"Yes, sir."

"Have a good trip, bucko. Solve the mystery and put all the ghosts to rest."

"Thanks, Dad. Signing off."

The time was 3:27.

Marco looked up Peter Edgar Masters's number in the phone book.

Pete had a habit of drawing a skull and crossbones on the back of his hand in class. He was also one of those people who, when Sister called the roll and everyone else answered, "Here, here, here," would announce, "Present." Then the whole class would laugh. Other than that, though, Pete was a good kid and a guy you could depend upon.

Marco dialed the number.

"Masters's Mansion," a rather squeaky voice answered.

"Pete?"

"Present."

"Marco here. Can you take my paper route for a few days? That would be tomorrow—Thursday—and also Friday, Saturday, and Sunday."

Counting them off on his fingers as he spoke, Marco realized that he had only four days—not much time to solve a mystery and put an uncertain number of ghosts to rest. Not much time at all.

"Sunday too, eh?" Pete asked. "That means getting up at like dawn. That'll cost you extra, buddy."

"Sure."

"You're off on another adventure," Pete remarked in an

envious tone as the clock ticked away. "Some guys have all the luck. . . ." Then he said, "Sure, Marco, ole buddy-buddy, I'll be glad to take over for you."

"Thanks, Pete. I'll leave the route book in the basket of my bike in the hall downstairs."

"Good hunting," Pete told him.

Marco ran to the hall closet, took out the suitcase, toted it to his room, and started to pack socks and pajamas and stuff. It occurred to him that this was the first real journey he had ever taken. What does a guy wear on his first journey?

Well, probably his best clothes. Marco put on a clean white shirt, his one tie, and his church coat and slacks. He guessed his loafers would do.

The time was 3:40.

What does a guy take in the way of personal possessions on his first journey—the first time he'd ever been on a train?

The boy gazed down at his treasure trove in the top drawer of the dresser:

A pocket flashlight; two shark's teeth; one of Marco's teeth; an Indian arrowhead; an Indian penny, dated 1887; an even dozen marbles, including a steely and a pair of cat eyes; a very powerful magnet; a Minié ball that he, personally, had dug out of a trench at Port Hudson, Louisiana, when his class had made a field trip to the Civil War battlefield and which he prized more highly than a gold nugget; a couple of retired Mexican jumping beans; a ball of neatly-wrapped rubber bands; a number of bottle caps in fair condition . . . and various other items of not much account.

Even though he'd like to, he couldn't bring them all, for he was traveling light. He hesitated a moment, then took the pocket flash, wrapped it in a T-shirt and closed the suitcase upon it. Then he phoned Western Union, and had a telegram sent to Shady Hall, reporting his time of arrival.

He was going out the front door when he remembered the route book.

3:45 on the nose.

Lugging the suitcase, Marco made his way to Royal Street and started toward the distant high buildings that he could glimpse through the iron balconies of the French Quarter. He walked for blocks . . . and blocks; but the tall buildings, like mountain peaks, on the other side of Canal Street appeared to be no closer. And he had a long way to go after he hit Canal.

As he hurried past the long line of antique shops on Royal, he seemed to see nothing but clocks in the windows. Each told a different time; some gave him a few minutes, others took them away; but all were in solemn-faced agreement that a very-well-dressed lad named Marco Fennerty was going to miss his train.

Forward, Marco Fennerty!

In desperation, the boy searched for a bus or a taxicab. Buses, there were none. There were plenty of cabs—all with passengers. A steady stream of cars was passing slowly, like a parade, or—the unpleasant thought came—a funeral procession.

Then, well behind him, the clock in the belfry of St. Louis Cathedral wound up and struck one, two, three, four. No, no, no, no, he was not going to make his train. . . .

"Hey, you! Where you think you're going?"

There at the curb was a perfectly beautiful police car, with that excellent fellow, Patrolman Snowman, at the wheel and a second fine-looking officer whom the boy didn't know beside him.

"Hi, Patrolman Snowman!" Marco exclaimed. "Going to Union Station. Got a train to catch."

"Lucky for you, we're off-duty and driving back to the garage that way. Hop in."

The clock in the belfry of St. Louis Cathedral struck four. He was not going to make his train!

Marco hopped in the back seat. The prowl car pushed out into the stream of traffic and, like a log, a barge, like a motorboat out of gas—was borne along to Canal Street in a most leisurely fashion as time, time, time went past at a gallop.

"Guess we'd better give 'em a growl," remarked Patrolman Snowman, a man who dearly loved to use the siren, bull horn, and other police gear.

Siren screaming, blue light flashing from the roof, radio sputtering, the prowl car rushed through the golden streets of New Orleans to Union Station. Marco hopped out of the back seat, thanked his two friends, and ran into the station with his suitcase.

He bought his ticket, then rushed to the train. A conductor stood on the platform, staring down at a big pocket watch as if mad at it. Marco knew exactly how he felt. Time was an enemy.

Clutching his suitcase, the boy climbed the steep, clanging, iron steps. The conductor waved to some buddy of his at the front of the train and followed Marco aboard, muttering to himself.

The car gave a lurch and banged into the one ahead of it, which banged into the next, which banged into the next—the next, the next—until the whole train seemed to be giving a long, noisy shudder. There was a hiss of steam from underfoot, along with an excited drumming sound, and the 4:17 pulled out of New Orleans. With a long mournful wail of its horn, the train began to pick up speed.

2

JOURNEY TO THE BEYOND

The tall, brown telephone poles flashed by the window like a long line of grenadiers standing guard.

"Keep a sharp lookout, lads," Marco ordered and gave them his best salute.

The train was racing past green, sunny fields, where horses and cows were thoughtfully munching grass and an occasional weed. The sun was like a Spanish doubloon and well above the trees—which was good. All things considered, it was best to arrive at Shady Hall before darkness set in.

Not, of course, that Marco Fennerty, Junior, was afraid of the dark. Huh! He was eleven-years-old and afraid of nothing. He was, as he remarked to himself from time to time, a boy without fear. A boy, who, as he also liked to tell himself, carried TNT in both fists.

He gazed down at his fist for a pleasant moment, then opened it and reached into his coat pocket for the letter from Lily. His "kissin' cousin." Huh!

He reread the letter:

Marco, there's something funny going on here. Aunt Hazel is scared to death but won't admit it 😠 I'm scared too but I admit it 🙂

The other faces on the page were like jack-o'-lanterns that lighted up the letter with their happy smiles. But the face Lily had drawn for the statement about her aunt made the boy shudder.

Or maybe it was just the train, as it went banging and clattering across Louisiana, away from home and friends. The clicking wheels reminded Marco of a ticking clock, then of the typewriter at the police station.

It sure would have been nice if Dad could have come along, it sure would. Besides being the bravest of the brave, Sergeant Fennerty was a mess of fun and also an expert splinter remover.

Time was slipping away with each tick of the wheels.

No longer did the sun resemble a Spanish doubloon. Bigger now and redder, it shone through the topmost branches of the trees, flashing like a blinker light as it raced the train through The Beyond. The neat, fenced-in pastures had given way to wide, brown marshes through which green bayous wandered, as if they had all the time in the world.

The sliding door at the front of the car rumbled open and the conductor shouted over the sudden roar of the train, "New Paris! New Paris!"

The next thing Marco knew, he was standing on the station platform with his suitcase. The conductor was shouting, "All aboard!" and the train was pulling out of New Paris with a sharp hiss of steam, and a long wailing question mark from its horn.

Smiling shyly, the boy glanced around, looking for his Cousin Lily and her Aunt Hazel. No one, however, was there to meet him.

Hmmm. He went into the dim, empty waiting room and walked over to the telephone booth. In the ragged phone book that dangled inside, he found "Danton James Terrebonne Rd," dropped a nickel in the slot and dialed the number:

No answer.

Well, well, well. Picking up his bag, Marco started for the town square. The clock in the tower of the faded brick courthouse there said 7:05.

The cast-iron soldier of the Confederate memorial stood on his granite pedestal, gazing across the street at the Magnolia Drugstore with his steady, iron eyes. On another corner, a Civil War cannon was pointed at the J. C. Penney department store.

Marco walked past the dusty, dark store windows till he came to the Western Union office, which was ablaze with light. Printing with great care, he wrote on the yellow telegram form:

ARRIVED SAFELY. REGARDS, MARCO.

As he paid the clerk, he asked, "Ma'am, can you tell me how to get to Shady Hall on Terrebonne Road?"

"Shady Hall!" she exclaimed. "You don't want to go *there*." She gave him a sharp glance over her spectacles. "Do you?"

"Yes, ma'am."

"You must be a very brave young man."

"Well," Marco murmured, his face burning, for he was in full agreement with this solid, gray-haired lady but didn't want to say so.

"A very brave young man, indeed." She shrugged her meaty shoulders. "Well, it's your funeral. Shady Hall, God bless you, is five miles from here. This street we're on becomes a gravel road about a mile out of town. The first left is a shell road—Terrebonne Road—and that takes you to Shady Hall, but I wouldn't go there if I were you, really I wouldn't."

"Thank you, ma'am," Marco told her. "Can I get a cab?"

"I doubt it," she replied. "Oh, we have a taxi service in New Paris," she added quickly. "But I expect Tad Payne would not care to go out to Shady Hall at this time of day, things being as they are. You can ask him, though. He's at the gas station right up the street."

"Thank you, ma'am."

"God bless you," the clerk said.

Glancing back as he went out the door, Marco saw her blessing *herself*.

As Marco walked up to the gas station, a tall man in greasy overalls ambled out of the dark cave of the garage, wiping his greasy hands on a greasy towel. He leaned against the gas pump.

"Right warm for September," the man said.

"Mr. Payne?" Marco asked.

"That's my name."

Tad Payne needed a shave in the worst way and had big black knuckles that he was in the habit of cracking. He slumped against the gas pump as if he really needed its support.

In the courthouse tower, the clock chimed the half-hour. Marco had the sudden feeling that the clock was telling the time of a warm September evening fifty years ago.

Nodding his head on its long neck toward the tower, Tad Payne remarked, "They used to hang people there in the old days." He added with an air of regret, "Not anymore, though."

Crack! went the black knuckles of his left hand.

"Mr. Payne?" Marco began.

"That's my name."

"Can you drive me out to Shady Hall?"

"Shady Hall!" Tad Payne's eyes grew narrow. "Why in the world would you want to go out there? And don't tell me it's none of my beeswax—I don't like smart kids."

It occurred to the boy, that it was *not* any of Mr. Payne's beeswax, but he answered, "I'm visiting my cousin and her aunt there. Can you take me?"

"I could, yes, I could," the man said slowly. "Whether I *would* or not is a different matter. A different matter altogether."

And *caar-rack!* went the knuckles of his right hand.

"What would you charge?" Marco asked.

The man did not answer. He appeared to be thinking.

"Please, sir, what's the fare?" the boy asked.

"The fare, yes, the fare. For you . . ."

Tad Payne's voice rose and his head cocked back on his neck. Then the head snapped forward like the hammer of a gun. "Ten dollars. You have that kind of money on you?"

"Yes sir, but isn't that sort of high?"

"No, friend, it isn't, and I'll tell you why right quick. Nobody in his right mind goes out to Bayou Terror after dark—nobody. And, as you can see, it's getting dark right now."

"Yes sir."

The sun had set in the back of The Beyond, leaving only a pink glow. In the south, the direction of the Gulf of Mexico, long, blue clouds were mustering like regiments of infantry preparing for a night assault.

"Okay," Marco agreed at last. "Can we get going?"

"Like I said, that'll be fifteen dollars."

"Fifteen!" the boy exclaimed.

"I'll be coming back empty," Tad Payne pointed out. "You can see my position, friend."

"I see your position," Marco replied. From the way Mr. Payne was leaning against the gas pump, if it broke off, he would go sprawling on the concrete. Mr. Payne, he decided, picking up his suitcase, was not a very nice guy.

"Where are you going?" the man called.

"The fare — ten dollars. Nobody in his right mind goes out to Bayou Terror after dark — nobody."

"Shady Hall," Marco answered over his shoulder.

"Ten dollars!"

Marco kept walking.

"Look out for the *loup-garou!*" the man yelled.

Who, Marco wondered, was Lou Garou? But he didn't ask.

Crack! went the blackened knuckles of Mr. Tad Payne.

By the time Marco had reached the gravel part of the road, he had shifted his suitcase from hand to hand seven different times. And it was totally dark, except for a full moon that sailed through the heavy storm clouds above, keeping an eye on him.

The trees, which had remained a respectful distance behind the guard line of telephone poles along the railroad track, now pressed in closely. They tossed their proud heads in the wind and hissed at him. Autumn leaves scrambled across the gravel at him like crabs. Other leaves rushed down at him, right at him, like swooping hawks.

Forward, Marco Fennerty—he of no fear!

City boy that he was, Marco yearned for streetlights, and the sounds of music and laughter and plates clattering. But in The Beyond the only sounds came from the noisy trees, and the dark was so *dark* in the darkness.

Had he thought he was traveling light? The suitcase felt as though he had packed a few cannon balls. For the—he did not know how-many-eth time—Marco shifted the bag to the other hand.

He had come to Terrebonne Road. It was a long, dismal tunnel of trees whose branches interlocked overhead, with ragged streamers of Spanish moss hanging down from them.

Left face! Forward, Fearless Fennerty!

Marco tensed his stomach muscles, as he did in the hall at school, when he thought a classmate might give him a playful punch passing by. Left, right, left, right—his loafers crunched on the oyster shells that paved the winding road.

Lightning bugs flared orange in the bushes ahead, like the gun flashes of a lost battle. A white moth, like a small and rather feeble bat, bobbed and bobbled ahead of him as if to show the way, and then—just like *that*—vanished.

The moon, an old, cold, gold piece, peeked at him from time to time through the trees. It was keeping up with him pretty well. But then, Marco thought, it didn't have a winding road to travel (over oyster shells), or a suitcase to lug along the way.

His heart was pounding, his throat dry. It would be a simple matter to set down the one-ton suitcase and open it—a flashlight was a good friend for a city boy in the country. . . .

That lump of darkness on his left that looked like a crouching grizzly, or a giant man-eating toad in urgent hunger —he knew was just a clump of bushes. That long terrible-looking thing that dangled from the branch up ahead was not a hanged pirate or highwayman—it was nothing in the world but a mess of leaves swinging from a stupid old vine.

Yes, he knew this, sure. Just the same, and however, and nonetheless, it would be a jolly thing to whip out the old flashlight. Then he could make certain before he had to pass these silly black phantoms, with his stomach in a large knot, and grasping the handle of the suitcase in one hand and TNT in the other.

But, no, and again, no! The flashlight would remain in the suitcase, where it belonged.

Wait! What was *that*?

From somewhere up ahead, there came a chilling cry. It started as a low, sad, yearning moan that grew louder and more sorrowful as it rose to a high pitch—hung there for a few shivery moments—then fell back to its low, mournful level before dying out completely.

In five quick movements, Marco dropped the bag, crouched, unzipped it, yanked out the flash, and swept the yellow beam across the road ahead. Bushes, trees, oyster shells —nothing else was to be seen.

Gungah! The eerie howl had hit him like a blow in the chest, prickling the hairs on the back of his neck. As he crouched there, wondering what to do, he felt a rush of wind, then heard a snapping spatter on the leaves around him. Rain!

Oh, great! Delightful! Now, on top of everything else, he was about to receive a thorough soaking in a good old Louisiana downpour. He zipped up the bag, and searched along the side of the road until he found a straight, heavy branch that would serve as a nice club in case that whatever-it-was attacked.

Then, with the club tucked under his arm, he marched forward, playing the flashlight back and forth ahead of him. The wild cry, fortunately, did not come again. The rain, however—the cold, wet rain—began to fall with gusto.

A gleam of light appeared on the telephone wires ahead, then a flare of green showed along the forest wall. Finally, Marco saw the headlights of an approaching car, the long, golden needles of rain rushing eagerly toward them.

The car shot past, tires hissing on the shells. Then it stopped, tail lights glowing red against the bushes, and backed up the road to him.

"Miss Danton?" Marco asked, peering through the darkness.

But the driver was a man, who said, "I see a boy walking along a country road, in the rain, with a suitcase as big as he is and I say, 'Something's wrong. Yes sir, something's wrong.' Get in, Son. I'll give you a lift."

"No, thank you, sir," Marco replied.

"It's all right, Son," the man assured him. "I'm Mortimer Slade, M.D. An old friend of Jim Danton's, poor soul, and his sister Miss Hazel. You must be going to Shady Hall. It's the only place you could be heading for on this road. Get in. I'll take you there. After all, what are friends for?"

"Well, I guess it's okay," the boy said. "Thank you, sir."

The inside of Dr. Slade's car looked as though some prankster had locked up a couple of unfriendly wildcats over a long week end. Everything was in shreds, and a spring in Marco's seat stuck up like a jack-in-the-box that had come out of his box.

"Make yourself comfortable," Dr. Slade told him, turning the car around. "You know, automobiles are just like people. You say, 'I don't feel good today. I've got a sore throat. My back aches. Automobiles are the same. They have to breathe. Sometimes they're a little cranky. And I'll tell you, this old crate of mine has let me know that we're in for some bad weather."

He glanced at the boy, and his big, white teeth gleamed in the dashlight as he smiled, repeating, "Bad weather."

"Yes, sir." Marco smiled back, for, to him, bad weather was good, as long as he wasn't out in it without the proper foul-weather gear.

They drove along the white road, with the windshield wipers swishing back and forth, and the headlights stabbing like swords through the rainy dark.

"Mortimer Slade, M.D.," Dr. Slade repeated, sticking out his right hand. As far as Marco could tell in the uncertain light, he seemed to be a youngish sort of man.

"Marco Fennery, Junior," the boy replied, shaking hands. "I'm visiting Shady Hall for a few days before school starts."

He hoped the man would not ask him if he liked school, since grownups had a way of doing this. But Dr. Slade remarked, "Well, you've picked an interesting time to be visiting Shady Hall. Strange things going on there now."

He gave Marco his gleaming smile. "*Right* strange. Downright spooky, from all I hear."

"The taxi driver wanted fifteen dollars to take me out there," the boy replied.

"That's Tad Payne for you," Dr. Slade remarked. "Always looking for the buck. But few are the people in New Paris who will go out to Bayou Terrebonne after dark. Few indeed. *Terrebonne* is French for *good land,* you know," he added, as if to change the subject.

"Tad Payne called it Bayou Terror," Marco said, watching the driver's face. Dr. Slade kept his eyes on the road. The windshield wipers were quite noisy in his silence.

"Well, yes," the doctor replied at last. "Bayou Terrebonne has an evil reputation. Shady Hall is supposed to be haunted and have some kind of curse on it. It had a long history of crime in the old days, you know. Smuggling, robbery, suicide, murder."

"Murder?" Marco repeated, thinking, *Gungah!*

"That's the story now," Dr. Slade told him carefully, as with the same attention, he guided the car around a wide bend in the road. "But you've got to understand these bayou people. They're a superstitious lot, and they've always resented the Dantons."

"Really?" Marco asked.

"They consider the Dantons uppity, you know, snobs— I'm just telling you what the *people* think," he went on in his careful way, "not what *I* think."

"Yes, sir," the boy said. "I understand."

"I'm sure you do," Dr. Slade agreed, "a bright young fellow like yourself. It's true that Miss Hazel has certain strange ways, and so did Mr. Jim—he passed on just a year ago, as I expect you were aware."

"Yes, sir."

"The people of New Paris were annoyed about his funeral arrangements—burial at dawn and all."

"Yes, sir."

"And they're also annoyed that Jim went off and got himself a Yankee lawyer in Washington, D.C., to draw up the will. Antoine Boudier, who had handled the Danton legal matters for years and years, wasn't good enough for him any-more—that's what the people say."

"I see," Marco replied, although he was getting a bit confused.

"Then the Yankee lawyer got everything in a mess. Serves Mr. Jim right, the people say. Of course, they're mostly mad that Jim didn't leave the town any money in his will—but why should he? That's what I'd like to know."

"Yes, sir."

"They say that Henri Cassatt—the bridge tender on Bayou Terrebonne—was really mad that Jim didn't leave him any-thing, after they'd been friends so long. Particularly when Jim left a considerable sum for the care of his cat."

The doctor's long teeth gleamed in the dashlights: "A considerable sum by New Paris standards. *Con-sid-er-a-ble.*"

"Say," Marco asked, "is the cat's name maybe Lou Garou?"

"Lou Garou?" Dr. Slade turned the question over in his scientific mind. "I, myself, have never heard Mr. Jim or Miss Hazel refer to him as anything but Curious Cat."

"Tad Payne told me to look out for Lou Garou," Marco said.

"Oh, he must meant the *loup-garou.*"

"Guess so," Marco agreed. "What's that mean?"

The rain had stopped, but the windshield wipers continued to patiently wipe the windshield. Dr. Slade turned with a gleam of teeth:

"Werewolf."

"Werewolf!"

The doctor nodded in firm agreement:

"Werewolf."

Gungah! Marco Fennerty, Junior, a fearless New Orleans boy of eleven years, found that both of his hands were clenched into fists, his stomach a much bigger fist.

"*Loup-garou,* from the Old French, taken from the original Latin, for *man wolf,*" explained Dr. Slade, a man who obviously enjoyed passing on information of all kinds. "You've got to understand these people," he went on. "Most of them are Acadians—French settlers who came to the bayou country around the middle of the eighteenth century, from a colony in Canada called Acadia. Hence, their name. Today these Acadians are known as Cajuns."

"Yes, sir," the boy said, thinking, *werewolf. Gungah!*

"The old beliefs of Europe from centuries and centuries ago still hold on here, Marco," Dr. Slade told him. "New Paris is not New Orleans."

"No, sir!"

"The people of the bayou country think that on the night of a full moon . . . such as tonight," the doctor added, ". . . a man who is so cursed—a man who, by day, might be the meekest, mildest person you ever saw, Marco—suddenly finds himself changing into a wolf."

The boy asked softly, "And he howls?"

"He howls," Dr. Slade agreed.

"Why?"

"The belief is that he is calling for his next victim."

Marco gazed down at his clenched fists, thinking TNT, TNT. He asked, "Do you believe all this, Doctor?"

"Ah, here we are at Bayou Terrebonne," Dr. Slade said.

Though the dark, somber trees and clumps of bushes lay a stretch of water that was all silvery in the moonlight.

Frogs, a thousand or more strong, were singing with great enthusiasm but with a certain lack of imagination, and their tiny eyes glittered green as the car headlights swept past them. The moon shone down upon the trees across the bayou. The ancient, monstrous oaks stretched out branches like muscular arms, from which the Spanish moss hung like torn gray clothes.

So this was Bayou Terror. It was easy enough to see why the people of New Paris did not come around here after dark.

"Doctor," Marco repeated, "do you believe in the were-wolf?"

"And here," said Dr. Slade, "is Shady Hall."

The headlights flashed on a great dark house that was almost invisible behind a high wall of bamboo. The boy could see the tops of a line of white columns and three gables sticking out from the slate roof, the windows and the roof aglow in the moonlight. So this was Shady Hall. It looked as if it had been deserted for a hundred years.

"Doctor Slade," the boy pointed out as the car crunched to a halt, "I asked you if you believed in the *loup-garou*."

"I was just telling you what the people around here believe," the doctor replied. "They use a raft of garlic since they think it protects them from the werewolf. Chew enough of that stuff, Son, and it'll keep *anything* away."

Dr. Slade's teeth gleamed, "Say, Marco, I hope I haven't frightened you with all this talk.'

"Huh! I am a boy of—of eleven years."

"Good lad!" the doctor replied. "Well, Marco, I'd come

in with you, but I'm on a call. Told Mrs. LaBlanc to bring the kids in for flu shots, but, no, she was too busy— and now they've *all* got the bug."

"Thanks very much for the ride, sir," the boy said, getting out.

"What are friends for?" Dr. Slade asked.

It occurred to Marco, as he started to carry his suitcase up the flagstone walk to the big dark house, that the doctor never had told him whether or not he believed in the *loup-garou*.

3

FACES IN THE FIRE

Shady Hall. Something about that place gave Marco a funny feeling in the pit of the stomach. It was not fear. What an *ab* (left) *so* (right) *lute* (left, right, left) *ly* silly idea!

But as he walked up the flagstones a sadness, a dreariness, about the house seemed to settle upon him. One small light burned in a downstairs room. It appeared to make the rest of that area darker, the upstairs gloomier.

Ragged black clouds were racing past the moon, sometimes blocking it out completely. But the mossy, mossy oaks, with their long arms and clutching fingers, kept Shady Hall in shadow. A wind from Bayou Terror pushed cooly against the boy's forehead, and roared softly around his ears, rattling the bamboo behind him like dry bones.

Something—a big, black something—shot in front of him.

Marco clenched his free fist. The moon came out like a spotlight, shining down on a big, black cat—as large as a small dog—crouched on a flagstone before him.

"*Merr-ow!*"

The animal ran forward five flagstones, stopped, humped like a black camel, glanced back at Marco with golden eyes and repeated, "*Merr-ow!*"

He ran forward six flagstones, turned to see if the boy was still following, and added, "*Merr-ow!*"

The pair had come to the front door. The cat reached

up, stretching, claws out, scratching on the wood. Then he crouched and leaped up upon the latch, remarking, "*Merr-ow!*"

With the animal riding it, the door slowly and rather noisily swung open. Then the cat sprang down and, without further comment, vanished in the darkness of the hallway.

Marco stood in the doorway, calling, "Lily? Miss Danton?"

There was no answer.

Like most houses, Shady Hall had a personality all its own. At once the boy felt the presence of the hundred and sixty years or so that this great dark place held, along with an awareness of all the Dantons who had lived here—and died here.

The house did not smell musty, however. Nor did it smell dusty. Miss Danton, he decided, must be an excellent house-keeper. But what a huge house to keep!

It had a pleasant, spicy smell, as though from the many thousands of good meals cooked here and the log fires that had blazed through the hundred and sixty or so winters.

He was standing at the end of a long, dark hall. At the other end he saw a faint light that apparently was coming from a room that led off the hall. He walked toward the light, the floor boards creaking with each careful step. He passed a tall grandfather clock, whose deep, slow ticktock seemed to command, "Not so fast there!"

Behind him the front door groaned briefly and shut with a bang.

Marco did not jump, not really. He stood for a moment, listening to his heart, to the clock, and to the noises that, he guessed, such an old place would just naturally make. Then there came to his ears a curious hissing sound, as if the house were breathing.

Yes sir, Shady Hall was sure a spooky place, filled with shadows and sighs and creaks and squeaks—a big, dark, de-

Marco did not jump, not really. He stood for a moment, listening to his heart, to the clock, and to the noises...!

lightful house altogether. Maybe it had a secret passage. Surely a house, this big, this old, this dark (with a curse on it) would have a hidden staircase or at least a sliding panel somewhere.

Tomorrow, he and Lily would have to check this out. The only trouble was, where in the world could Lily—and her great-aunt—be now?

The light came from the kitchen. Something that smelled good, mighty good indeed, was popping and plopping in a big iron pot on the stove. Under the stove, the black cat was quietly polishing off a bowl of cream. He glanced up at the boy politely, asked, *"Merr-ow?"* and went back to his cream.

From outside sounded the hungry crunch of tires on oyster shells, and the slam blam of two car doors.

"Lily," the voice of what was evidently a grown-up woman came, "you run ahead and turn off the chicken. I'll put in a call to New Orleans."

The kitchen door opened and a stocky girl in blue jeans burst into the room, her long blonde hair flying behind her. Then sneakers squealed to a halt on the floor, round tan arms swung forward; hair flew in the same direction; small, tan hands pushed the sun-bleached locks back from big, blue eyes.

"Marco!" the girl gasped. "What're you doing here?"

"Hi, Lily," the boy greeted her. "Waiting for y'all," he explained.

"He's here, Aunt Hazel! Marco's here!" Lily called. "Say, boy," she demanded, "why weren't you at the station?"

"I was," Marco replied. "Where were you?"

"Wait a minute, wait a minute—you must have got off the train at the station in *New Paris!*" Lily exclaimed, and the boy admitted that such was the case.

"We expected you at Terrebonne," Miss Danton told him, coming into the kitchen. "It's a little country station, much closer to us and the one the Dantons have always used. I should have realized—not thinking too clearly. But never mind, you're here. Welcome to Shady Hall, Marco."

"Thank you, ma'am."

Miss Danton was tall, very tall; and thin, much too thin. She reminded the boy of one of those stalks of bamboo that closed off the front yard.

Her hair had been red once, and some of it still was, but the rest was gray, turning white. She had a weary, haggard look, as though she had not enjoyed a good night's sleep in months.

Her pale green eyes flashed restlessly around the room, as if she expected something—something bad—to happen at any moment.

"Now that's all settled, let's eat," suggested Lily, a frisky girl who burned up a good many calories in the course of a day.

They ate in the dining room, at a long dark table under a glittering chandelier. The walls were stained with age, and there was a big hole in the ceiling where plaster had fallen. But Marco pretended not to notice, concentrating on supper. The main dish was chicken and thick, chewy noodles in a rich red sauce.

"This is *some* good," the boy told Miss Danton.

"It's the garlic that gives it such a nice flavor," she replied with a pleased smile.

"Garlic?"

"We use right much in these parts," she told him.

"That's what Dr. Slade said," he remarked, attacking a drumstick.

Miss Danton laid down her fork. "Where did you see him?"

"He gave me a ride to Shady Hall," Marco answered. "He

said the people here use garlic to protect themselves from the *loup-garou*."

"That little gossip!"

"Aunt Hazel!" her niece exclaimed, spearing a noodle.

"Well, he is," Miss Danton insisted. "I just wish he'd mind his own business, that's all. What else did that gossip tell you, Marco?"

There was a soft tapping at the window, and Miss Danton jumped.

"Rain," Marco told her.

It came in steady, insistant snaps, like the pecking of a flock of tiny birds.

"Dr. Slade said we're due for some bad weather," the boy remarked. "He said it twice. 'Bad weather.' "

"He's right there," Miss Danton replied. "We heard on the six o'clock news that there are storm warnings up from Galveston, Texas, to Mobile, Alabama. Hurricane Inez is out in the Gulf of Mexico and might hit anywhere along the coast."

"Oh, boy, I hope it hits here!" Lily exclaimed, glancing at her cousin, and he grinned to show his agreement.

"Marco, what else did the old gossip tell you?" Miss Danton repeated.

"Oh, let's see. He said that Shady Hall had a long history of crime in the old days."

"He did, did he? Well, Marco, you should know that every old family has a skeleton or two in the closet."

"Skeleton or two. *Gungah!*"

"I mean, every old family has some things in its history of which the members aren't proud," she explained.

"Yes, ma'am," the boy replied, thinking what a clever way it was for her to say that!

"You must realize, Marco, that when my great-great

grandfather built Shady Hall, this was frontier country—wild and lawless. The story goes—and I expect it's true enough—that this house was once a frontier inn. The Dantons were supposed to have been in cahoots with robbers and to have done business in smuggled goods with Jean Lafitte."

"Jean Lafitte!" the boy exclaimed.

"Yes, the famous buccaneer." Miss Danton nodded.

"Tell him about the tunnel, Aunt Hazel," her grand-niece urged, leaning forward eagerly.

Tunnel, Marco thought. *Gungah*! That beat a secret passage, any day.

"Yes, there *was* a tunnel from the cellar of Shady Hall to Bayou Terrebonne—"

"For the smugglers to bring the stuff in," Lily broke in.

"That's the *story*," her great-aunt stated firmly. "*We* say that the tunnel was for escape in case of an Indian attack. Anyhow, my great-grandfather sealed it up during the War Between the States, to keep the Yankees from using it. Then he and his two sons went off to join the Confederate Army, leaving my great-grandmother at Shady Hall all alone."

"All alone?" Marco asked.

"Except for a dozen or so loyal servants." Miss Danton shrugged. "He and one of the boys were killed in action at Champion's Hill, Mississippi, in 1863. The other son died of wounds during the siege of Vicksburg, later that year. It was a sad war for the Dantons, Marco."

"Yes, ma'am," the boy replied, adding to himself, and for a mess of other people, too.

"During the Red River Campaign, in the spring of 1864, Union gunboats steamed up Bayou Terrebonne and fired upon Shady Hall—there's still an unexploded shell stuck in one of the chimneys—we'll show it to you tomorrow."

"Great!"

"Union troops later occupied Shady Hall. My great-grand-mother went up to her bedroom and refused to come out as long as there was a single, solitary Yankee in her house. During the winter of 1864-65, Marco, she died of pneumonia in that room. The fireplace there never did work a hoot after that Yankee shell hit the chimney."

"I see."

"Tell him about the money, Aunt Hazel," her grand-niece urged.

"Money?" Marco repeated.

"Oh, the old gossip didn't mention that?" Miss Danton asked. "I wonder why. Anyway, the story is that there's a big pile of money hidden in Shady Hall, but it's all nonsense. Nonsense! In the South, every old house is supposed to have money hidden in it. But if there ever *was* any money, those thieving Yankees made off with it."

The pecking of the rain on the windows grew to a constant rattle. Wind moaned around the house and the lights in the chandelier overhead flickered . . . went out . . . then came back on again. . . .

"It's really too bad my brother Jim is no longer here," Miss Danton told Marco as the three were doing the supper dishes in the kitchen. "He could have told you much more about Shady Hall than I can. You would have liked Jim, Marco. He was the finest person I've ever known. And how that man loved this house!"

She stood like a tower, gazing off into space, then, with a quick movement, hung the dishcloth on the rack. She added, almost to herself, "Why, I'll never know."

Marco exchanged a glance with his cousin, then turned back to the Mistress of Shady Hall. He asked softly, "You don't like this house?"

She gazed down at him with her nervous green eyes. "No,

Marco, I don't. . . . In fact," she went on, "I hate it."

The wind moaned, as if in pain, and the rain spitter-spatter-splattered against the kitchen windows.

"I see," the boy said politely, although he didn't. Not at all.

Miss Danton gave him a quick smile. "Let's go into the study and have a fire," she suggested.

"A fire! Oh, boy!" Lily exclaimed.

"A fire!" Marco repeated. "*Gungah!*"

The study was a small, square room—a cozy room—with bookcases filled with books, and books (and books), reaching from the floor right up to the ceiling. An old desk stood in one corner. A pair of doors led out to the back of the house, facing Bayou Terrebonne. The rain dashed and splashed against two narrow windows on each side of the black marble fireplace, where logs had already been laid.

The study, Marco decided, was an ideal place in which to do your homework, or whatever it was that you wanted to study.

"This was Jim's favorite room," Miss Danton told Lily and Marco, bending down to light the fire. "When he left Shady Hall to the National Trust in his will, he insisted that the study—with all its books and papers—be kept exactly as it is."

The three pulled easy chairs up to the fire, which already was popping and snapping away, as if it knew its business.

"Miss Danton?" Marco began.

"Make it Hazel instead of Danton," she told him. "I'm not ashamed of my last name, but somehow 'Miss Danton' makes me sound like an old maid—which I am, it's true enough, but I'd rather not be reminded of it."

"Miss Hazel," the boy went on, "what's the—that thing you said?"

"The National Trust for Historic Preservation," Miss Hazel told him, "is an organization in Washington, D.C., that restores old places like Shady Hall to their original glory so visitors can come from all over and wander through the rooms and see how the people of the United States once lived."

Miss Hazel seemed to shiver—or maybe it was just the flicker of the flames on her thin, white, tight face.

"Your brother didn't leave Shady Hall to you in his will?" Marco asked politely.

It definitely was not the flickering flames. Miss Danton shivered, although the room was quite warm. She jumped up and went over to jab at the blazing logs with a poker.

"I didn't *want* Shady Hall," she told him. "When he willed the house to the National Trust, Jim planned to leave me enough money to live comfortably wherever I wanted. And just as soon as everything gets straightened out, I'm going to leave this awful place and move to Florida and get me some sun."

"Shady Hall *awful?*" the boy asked in surprise.

"Oh, Marco, you don't know the half of it!" Lily exclaimed, hugging herself.

"Well, I'd like to," he replied.

She raised one finger as if to say, "Tell you later."

"*Merr-ow!*"

"Ah," Miss Hazel said, "here's Curious Cat. There's nothing he doesn't know about this place, *nothing*. He's into everything. Marco, if he could only talk!"

Curious Cat stalked into the study like a shrunken black panther. He walked slowly and carefully over to the boy's chair, gazed up at him, then jumped into his lap, happily sighing, "*Merr-ow.*"

Marco had never thought much about cats—except tigers —really. He liked all animals—tigers, horses, dogs, otters, antelopes, jaguars, hyenas—well, *maybe* hyenas—but he knew nothing about cats. He had never owned one, and this was the first time he could remember that he'd had one in his lap.

The boy scratched behind the animal's sharp little ears. He remembered fondly Tiger, the Royal Bengal, he had once owned and still visited, as often as he could at the zoo in New Orleans.

"Miss Hazel," Marco said, "Dr. Slade told me that Shady Hall has a curse on it."

Curious Cat shook his head so hard his ears snapped. It was as though he were saying, "No, no, no!"

Miss Danton put down the poker and went back to her chair.

"The story *is* that Shady Hall is cursed," she told him. "All the townspeople believe it, but I think it's too silly even to talk about."

Marco stroked Curious Cat under his chin. "*Merr-ow.*" Ah, that was more like it! He lay stretched across the boy's knees like a thousand-dollar fur piece, purring like a $1.98 electric clock.

"Mr. Cooper says a few other old houses in this section of the country were supposed to be cursed at one time or another," Miss Hazel went on, "but that it doesn't mean a thing."

"Mr. Cooper?" the boy asked. "Who's Mr. Cooper?"

"Calvin Cooper. He's a Negro man who works for the U.S. Army Corps of Engineers. He's down here making a flood control study on Bayou Terrebonne for the Engineers. And he's absolutely fascinated with the old plantation houses in the Deep South. What that man doesn't know about American history and architecture! He has earned degrees from Harvard and the University of Chicago, and I don't know what all!"

"Aunt Hazel is letting him and his son stay in the cottage on the grounds here, back of the house," Lily said. "You'll like his son, Marco. And he has a big dog."

"Mr. Cooper has gone to make his report to the Division Engineer at Vicksburg," Miss Danton told him. "He should be back tomorrow. You'll have to talk with him, Marco. Smartest man!"

"I'd like to meet him," the boy said. "Miss Hazel, when will the National Trust people start working on Shady Hall?"

"I don't rightly know," she replied. "There has been some sort of mix-up"

Curious Cat laid his paw on Marco's arm, as if to say, "Now get this."

"Dr. Slade said the lawyer in Washington messed up the will or something," the boy said.

"Dr. Slade, Dr. Slade, Dr. Slade!" Miss Hazel exclaimed. "If that man would spend more time keeping people well, and less time gossiping, we'd all be better off"

Marco stroked Curious Cat, exchanging a glance with Lily.

"People in town are mad because Jim didn't use Antoine Boudier to make the arrangements with the National Trust," Miss Hazel explained.

"Yes," the boy agreed. "That's what—" He caught himself in time. "That's what I thought."

Miss Hazel gave him a sharp look with her nervous eyes.

"Whatever the reason," she went on, "there's been a mix-up. It appears that Jim didn't have as much money as he had reckoned."

"I don't understand," the boy told her. "Does that mean that the National Trust won't take the house or something?"

"I don't know, Marco. It's a very complicated matter." She gave him a quick smile. "Maybe your friend Dr. Slade will explain it all to us tomorrow."

The logs must have been put in the fireplace at the end of

last winter and had remained there all those long months, wait-ing for such a wild night as this. One fell to the hearth with a quiet crash and a flurry of sparks, leaving the two others on the andirons. They lay side by side, popping and flaring like enemy men-of-war, masts shot away, firing into each other.

"*Merr-ow!*"

Curious Cat stood up, stretched, jumped off Marco's lap and walked stiff-legged to the door. "*Merr-ow!*" he remarked. "*Rrrow!*" he added to make his point clear.

"He wants out," Miss Hazel said.

Marco opened the door. Wet wind rushed into the room. Curious Cat paused thoughtfully in the doorway as a number of cold raindrops smacked the boy in the forehead. Then, with a "*Merr-ow,*" the animal was gone in the night darkness.

Marco returned to his seat before the fire, which was dying. One of the remaining logs was down by the stern, blue and yellow flames fluttering from the bow. Boldly, shadows were slipping into the room.

"Miss Hazel," Marco asked, "what's wrong with Shady Hall?"

She gazed into the fire as if trying to see faces in the glow-ing logs. Wind moaned down the chimney, chasing a fright-ened puff of smoke into the room.

"You know what Winston Churchill said?" she replied. "'We shape our buildings, then our buildings shape us.'"

"What's that supposed to mean?" Lily asked.

Miss Hazel turned to the boy. "Do you know, Marco?"

He thought it over. "I guess he meant that, after we build, like a house, and live in it awhile, it has some kind of effect on us."

"Exactly," Miss Hazel told him. "Our lives are formed by the places we've lived in. I've spent most of my life in Shady Hall and, believe me, somebody living in a little shack in New

Paris has no reason to envy me in this 'stately old mansion,' as everyone calls it."

Marco and his cousin exchanged glances.

"Miss Hazel, you don't think Shady Hall is haunted, do you?"

Miss Danton stared into the fire, and the boy followed her gaze. The defeated, sinking man-of-war had changed into a dragon, breathing flame from its open, jagged jaws.

"Haunted?" Miss Hazel repeated slowly. "I think, Marco, that a house this old—a house where so many people of the same family have lived such violent and tragic lives—is bound to hold some traces of them somehow. But I've never seen a ghost, if that's what you mean."

"I guess that's what I mean," the boy replied, not quite sure what he meant.

"It's far, far easier to *feel* the past than to *hear* it," she went on. "It's far, far easier to *hear* it than to *see* it."

"And, brother, we've heard some funny things!" Lily exclaimed. "And I don't mean funny ha-ha."

The dragon had changed to a sharp-toothed rat, with a single red eye glittering at them.

"What kind of things?" Marco asked softly.

His cousin hugged herself, and her eyes got big.

"Footsteps and thumping and . . . and . . ."

Outside, in the dark wet night there came that eerie cry that Marco had heard earlier. It was closer now, much louder, much eerier. It started as a moan that climbed up and up to an almost painful howl, which seemed to rattle the windows, then sank to a sad moan that could have been the wind. . . . Like the wind, it died away to a hushed silence.

4

THE FOOTPRINT

Lily gasped. Marco felt as though he had taken a long drink of ice water. Miss Danton's fingers clamped on the boy's arm like claws. Her face was deathly white in the flickering flames as the cry came once more, then a third time. The three sat in the shadowy room, listening.

But the cry did not come again. The next sound they heard was completely different.

"*Merr-ow!*"

"That's Curious Cat, Marco," Miss Hazel said. "Let him in, please—quickly."

The boy ran to the bayou doors and yanked one open.

A huge shape with gleaming eyes lunged out of the night, bounding into the room. Miss Danton's and Lily's screams sounded as one. Marco's fists grasped TNT.

"Oh!" Lily exclaimed . . . then added, "Tolliver!"

Tolliver was a big, golden Labrador retriever. He bounced around the room, tail wagging furiously, sniffing, snorting. His upper lip flapped while he panted "*huh, huh, huh,*" as if amused at some private joke.

Marco let go the TNT, swallowing with some difficulty. "'The little dog laughed to see such sport,'" he recited.

"'And the dish ran away with the spoon!'" Lily replied with a nervous giggle.

Behind Marco there came a soft, quick, knock-knock-knock at the door.

Marco whirled about and saw a boy several years older than he, and much, much bigger than he, standing in the doorway.

"Anybody here seen my dog?" the boy asked.

"Eugene Gerard!" Miss Hazel exclaimed. "Come in. That dog of yours just scared the life out of us!"

"I heard the howling and let him loose to scout around," the boy explained, coming into the room.

"Eugene Gerard," Miss Hazel introduced him, "this is Marco Fennerty, Junior, all the way from New Orleans."

"Howdy, Eugene," Marco said, putting out his hand.

"Eugene Gerard," the boy corrected, shaking hands. "The last name is Cooper."

Eugene Gerard was a big, tall guy—about thirteen or fourteen, Marco figured—who looked as though he had been doing pushups every morning upon arising since the age of seven and a half. He took off his raincoat, leaving it by the doorway. He was wearing faded blue jeans, and a white T-shirt that seemed to make his dark, muscular arms even darker.

"Eugene Gerard is Mr. Cooper's son," Miss Hazel explained.

"Thought so," Marco replied, and the two boys shook hands again.

"Something's out there, man," Eugene Gerard told him. "Want to have a look?"

"Let me get my flashlight and rain gear."

For the first time, Eugene Gerard smiled. His teeth were as white as his T-shirt.

"I'm going, too!" Lily exclaimed.

"No, you are not, Miss Priss," her great aunt replied.

"Aunt Hazel!"

Tolliver bounded out into the night, leading the way, with his tail wagging like a flag. He was still chuckling, "*huh,*

huh, huh," at that private joke of his. The rain had stopped
for a bit, but the trees were so full of water and so full of leaks
that the drops came down steadily, falling in quick yellow
darts through the long beam of the flash.

The wind had torn the black clouds overhead apart, like
an old blanket, and the stars—thousands and thousands of tiny,
bright lights—glowed in the deep blue sky.

"Hey, Eugene Gerard," Marco called, "imagine if you
had to count every star up there!"

"Yeah, man, and then—after you'd counted every last one
—somebody said, 'Sorry, you missed a few there. Start over,
slow.'"

The two boys grinned at each other in the starlight, as
they removed their rain gear to make their search easier.

"Merr-ow!"

Swinging the flashlight about, Marco found Curious Cat
crouched on a branch of a nearby magnolia tree. The boy
went over to the trunk, which was as straight and smooth as
the leg of an elephant. There, between two gnarled roots, as if
caught between the elephant's toes, something showed in the
mud.

"Hey, Eugene," Marco called, "a footprint!"

"That's Eugene Gerard," his new friend corrected him.
"Say there now—a footprint it is!"

The two boys peered down with great excitement at the
big imprint of a bare foot that showed in the light of the flash.

"It's got to be a fresh one," Marco pointed out. "If it had
been made much earlier, the rain would have washed it away
by now. It's a clue!"

"A clue it is. Evidence. Come on, my father has some
plaster of Paris in the cottage. We'll mix up a batch, pour it
into the footprint, and then we'll have something to show the
sheriff tomorrow!"

To talk about mixing up a batch of plaster of Paris, is one thing, however. To actually make a batch that could be poured into a footprint is something else altogether—as the two boys discovered after they had used up most of the plaster of Paris in the bag, and all the pots in the cottage.

No sooner had they dumped the glittering white powder into a pot, added cold water from the kitchen sink, and stirred a few times, than the plaster hardened like stone.

Paris, Marco decided when the third spoon had stuck fast in the third and last pot, must be an awfully rocky place.

"*Hmmm*," Eugene Gerard remarked. "Tell you what, man, we'll take the stuff out there in this bowl, pour in the water from this pitcher on the spot, give her a couple of whirls with this spoon, and dump her into the old clue before she has a chance to harden."

"I'm with you, man," Marco told him.

With Marco carrying the bowl of powder and Eugene Gerard toting the pitcher of water and the spoon, the detective agency of Fennery & Cooper returned to the scene of the evidence.

"Hey!"

"Where'd it go?"

Wherever it went, the footprint was gone! In its place were a number of paw prints that could have come from a dog—and could have come from a wolf!

"Eugene Gerard," Marco said, "you've heard about the werewolf, haven't you—the *loup-garou*?"

"Of course I have."

"What do you think about it?" Marco asked.

The black boy gazed down at the white boy from the grand height he had reached in thirteen or fourteen years.

"What do *you* think?"

"Dr. Slade said the old beliefs of Europe hold on here in

The two boys peered down with great excitement at the big imprint of a bare foot that showed in the light of the flash.

the bayou country," Marco told him. "Me, I'm a city boy."

"Me, too."

"So what do you think about the *loup-garou*?"

"I think it's just so much superstitious nonsense," Eugene Gerard declared. "How about you?"

"I expect you're right," Marco agreed. "But what happened to the footprint?"

"Probably while we were in the cottage, fooling around with that plaster of Paris mess, the fella that left the footprint came back and rubbed it out. He must have been hiding somewhere close and heard us talking about it. We weren't exactly whispering, you know."

"Where did these paw prints come from, do you think?" Eugene Gerard gazed down at him.

"I think they came from a dog that goes under the name of Tolliver."

As if in answer to his name, Tolliver came bounding up from the direction of Bayou Terror, still chuckling to himself He went straight to the magnolia and stood up on his hind legs, front paws resting on the trunk, and looked up the tree with interest.

"*Merr-ow!*"

"Curious Cat!" Marco exclaimed. "I'd forgotten about you. Wait a minute and I'll get a ladder and bring you down. Eugene Gerard," he went on, "where do you figure the howling comes from?"

"From a dog that goes under the name of Tolliver," the other boy repeated.

"Why does he howl, do you think?" Marco asked.

Eugene Gerard was watching his partner closely in the light of the flash.

"They say a dog howls when somebody is going to die."

"That's just an old superstition," Marco told him.

"Right, pal. Right! Now you're getting some sense."

"But why does he howl?"

"Why? Because it makes him feel good, that's why. Try it sometime."

Marco glanced up at the other boy, unsure whether he was teasing or not. He seemed to be serious, but you could never tell about a guy of thirteen or fourteen when he was talking to a guy of eleven.

"Tell me this, Marco," his friend said. "You heard the howling tonight—did you hear anything before it?"

"No," the younger boy told him. "What do you mean?"

"You didn't hear a sort of a humming sound just before the first howl?"

"A humming sound?" Marco repeated. "Of course, the wind was blowing. Maybe you heard the wind."

"This didn't sound like any wind," Eugene Gerard said flatly. "I've heard it before when Tolliver started his serenade, but never this clear." He shrugged his broad shoulders. "Anyhoo."

"*Merr-ow!*" Curious Cat was getting impatient.

"Marco!" Lily called from the study door. "Aunt Hazel says to come in—it's getting late!"

"Right with you!" The boy started to go for a ladder. "See you, Eugene Gerard."

"See you, Marco." The other boy replied, taking Tolliver toward the cottage and his doghouse.

With a "*Merr-ow!*" and several strong "*Rrrows*," Curious Cat came down the trunk of the magnolia headfirst, raced across the yard, and slipped through the study doorway.

Marco's room was on the second floor, at the end of the hall and overlooking Bayou Terrebonne. It was indeed getting late. The little clock ticking away on the night stand by the bed gave the time as 10:15. The boy folded his clothes over the back of an easy chair in the corner, put on his pajamas, turned off the light, lay back in the cool, clean-smelling sheets, and waited for sleep to come.

It wouldn't come. He tried a number of tricks he knew to bring it on, like counting by fives to 555, taking deep breaths, and pretending he was going for a long, slow swim in the warm waters of the Gulf of Mexico. Nothing, nothing, nothing worked.

Downstairs, the big grandfather clock in the hall rather grumpily chimed eleven, and then what seemed a good three hours later it struck midnight.

Gungah! Here it was a new day beginning, and he wasn't even through with the old one yet.

Marco lay in the dark room and listened to the creaking, complaining noises an old house makes as it settles down for the night. Then, once more, he heard that strange, soft hissing sound, as if the house were giving a long, tired sigh. Downstairs, the grumpy grandfather clock announced that it was 12:30—time everyone was asleep.

The boy, in full agreement, yawned drowsily. Then he heard another noise—a long, low, sad humming that seemed to come from a great distance. It sounded again, and again. It was . . . It was—of course!—the horn of a train.

And yet, Tolliver did not howl. Marco arose and went to the window. The moon had slipped out from behind the dark, speeding clouds, as if for a final check before going off duty. The bayou, the cottage, the doghouse—all seemed to be painted silver in the moonlight, which also poured through the window into the bedroom.

Dogs, it was said, sometimes howled at the moon, as did coyotes and wolves. Why?

The boy thought of Tiger and how he used to roar during thunderstorms. But that had been different. . . .

Once again, why did dogs, coyotes, wolves—and perhaps foxes—howl at the moon?

"Because it makes them feel good," Eugene Gerard would probably say. He *had* said, "Try it sometime."

Very well. Marco glanced about him shyly and cleared his throat. Then, his head raised, eyes fixed on the glowing moon, the boy took a deep breath, opened his mouth wide and howled:

"Oo-oooh!"

"*Merr-ow!*"

Curious Cat shot three feet straight up from the easy chair. He landed with a thump on the floor, leaped upon the bed, raced around and around it, launched himself into space, hit one wall, bounced off, hit another, then tore out the open doorway and scrambled down the hall, screaming at the top of his lungs, "*Merr-ow! Merr-ow! Merr-ow!*"

When he had recovered from his shock, Marco gave a dry laugh. He guessed that sometime after the light had gone out, Curious Cat must have slipped into the room and curled up in the easy chair—maybe his favorite sleeping place. That was one spot, the boy decided, going back to bed, that would not have the pleasure of old Curious Cat's company for quite a spell.

Marco snuggled in the bed. Outside, the wind moaned, hurling big, hard raindrops against the window. The house creaked and sighed. From downstairs, the grandfather clock told him in no uncertain terms that it was one o'clock. And then the boy heard no more. . . .

5

IF CURIOUS CAT COULD TALK

Marco opened sleepy eyes. Warm, yellow sunlight filled the room. It was the start of the first day of his visit to Shady Hall. He glanced at the little clock on the night stand: 6:10.

Too early to get up. The bed sure felt good. He dozed off; and, when he awoke again, the clock said it was ten minutes after six. No rush, he thought, closing his eyes in contentment. Time seemed to move so much slower in the country. Still 6:10.

But wait a minute—wait a minute!

Marco's eyelids snapped open like released window shades. He sat up straight in the bed and vaulted himself out onto the floor. The stupid clock had stopped. *Because*, he told himself angrily as he washed hastily, threw off his night clothes and pulled on his day clothes, you forgot to wind it last night.

Something good was cooking downstairs. Marco followed his nose to the kitchen, where Lily and her great aunt were getting breakfast.

"Good afternoon," his cousin greeted him dryly.

"Now, Lily, it's not even ten o'clock yet," Miss Danton told her. "Did you sleep well, Marco?"

"I guess so," the boy replied, stretching.

From her white, weary face, it was evident that Miss Hazel had hardly slept at all. But she gave him a smile, putting a plate with bacon and two fried eggs sunny-side-up at his place. The eggs—like the round, yellow eyes of an owl—seemed to gaze up at him.

"I had a *terrible* night," Lily told the other two with a good deal of satisfaction. "I had *just* dropped off to sleep when Curious Cat ran past my door, screaming like crazy."

"Yes, I heard him, too—I wonder what in the world could have frightened him so," Miss Hazel remarked.

"I heard him, too," the boy told his eggs softly.

"Then everything's quiet for a while," Lily went on. "But then the *howling* starts."

"Yes," her aunt agreed, eyes darting around the room. "It seemed to be worse last night than it has ever been."

"I didn't hear a thing," Marco told them rather guiltily.

"You wouldn't!" Lily said.

"Miss Hazel, you know it's Tolliver that's doing all the howling, don't you?" the boy asked.

"Yes, I know there's no *loup-garou*," she answered with a tired smile. "Just the same, it gets on the nerves after a spell."

"Miss Hazel, did you hear any other sound each time before he howled?"

"Now that you mention it, Marco, I did hear something."

"What did it sound like?"

"I don't rightly know. The wind kept blowing through the trees and the rain made quite a commotion—but, once or twice before the howling, it did seem to me that I heard a sort of buzz."

"A humming?"

"Yes, I reckon you could call it a humming. Why? What is it? What does it mean?"

A tinge of color came into her cheeks, and her smile no longer was tired as she waited for his answer. Marco dropped his eyes.

"I'm sorry, I don't know, ma'am. Eugene Gerard told me

he has heard a humming before Tolliver lets go. I heard a train horn last night—it didn't make Tolliver howl, though."

"Anyway," Miss Danton told the others as they did the breakfast dishes, "it appears we're going to have us a nice day. I heard on the nine o'clock news that Hurricane Inez is heading west."

"Then it won't hit here!" Lily exclaimed. She and Marco groaned with disappointment.

"It might, children, it might," Miss Hazel told them soothingly. "Like any woman, Inez can't make up her mind."

"Hey," Marco asked, "has anyone seen Curious Cat this morning?"

His cousin shook her head. Miss Hazel said, "Sure haven't. But he's around somewhere, never fear."

The boy hoped he hadn't frightened the animal away for good with his howl. Apparently, Curious Cat was used to the Tolliver variety.

"Lily," Marco said when the dishes were done, "let's check the backyard for clues."

"I'm with you."

Eugene Gerard and Tolliver were not at home. The grass that covered most of the yard was soaked, as if the bayou had risen during the night and flooded it. A great deal of the area where the grass didn't grow was a series of puddles—except for one small spot that the magnolia tree had sheltered from the rain.

On the edge of the bare patch was what looked like a footprint.

"Say, that looks like a footprint!" Lily exclaimed, coming over.

"It certainly does," the boy agreed. "And it is. Only trouble is, somebody else came along and stepped on it in the dark last night. AND . . ."

He compared the bottom of his loafer with the sharp ridges of the tread that blotted out the toes, and all the rest of the interesting part of the footprint . . .

"That someone else," he went on, "is a brainless lad who goes under the name of Marco Fennerty, Junior!"

He hauled off and slapped himself on the forehead, hard. He could not have done a better job if he had stomped upon the print on purpose.

"Come on, let's go back in," Lily urged. "We can sit in the study and talk."

Marco gave that dumb head of his another whack and followed her inside.

Last night's fire was a pile of gray ashes now, with a few stubborn red coals that refused to give up the fight. By day, the study was jollier than last night—but not much. It still had a quiet, serious look. It was not a place where you laughed or raised your voice.

Marco walked slowly around the room.

"What's today—Thursday?" he asked.

Lily nodded. "All day."

"Almost the end of the week," the boy remarked. "Isn't it funny about time? On Monday you think, oh, boy, the whole week to go. Then Tuesday comes and you think, okay, no hurry, still most of the week yet. Wednesday—still plenty of time. But then Thursday's here, and the week's almost over."

"Uh-huh," Lily replied, fiddling with her hair.

"Same with the year," Marco went on. "Summer seems to go on and on forever, but school starts in a few days. After that, there's Halloween, then Thanksgiving, then Christmas— and the year's over!"

"Uh-huh."

Marco Fennerty, Junior, that well-known partner in the detective agency of Fennerty & Cooper, halted his pacing. He gave himself a third and final swat on the forehead.

"Will you stop that?" Lily demanded. "You're going to make yourself slap-happy!"

Hands swinging at his sides, Detective Fennerty resumed his nervous pacing around the study.

With the help of the light that poured through the windows, he noticed things he hadn't been aware of last night—such as the old red shawl lying like a tent across Miss Hazel's chair and the huge, blind eye of the television set in the corner across from the desk. Neither of which, he thought, could be considered clues.

He studied the books on the shelves. Among many others was a set of Charles Dickens's novels, along with another set of the works of Sir Walter Scott. There were also a number of books on coins and some others on the supernatural, besides quite a few leather-bound volumes that looked as though they were diaries, business journals—that sort of thing.

"Hey, Lily, you think Jim Danton read all these books?" the boy asked. "Bet he did. You know, you could find out just what kind of a person a guy is by studying the books in his library."

"Uh-huh."

His cousin tossed her hair back as if throwing it away.

"Marco, listen: Aunt Hazel and I came back from shopping about three weeks ago, and found all the books in this room off the shelves, scattered all over the floor!"

"No kidding."

"No kidding. All over the floor. You never saw such a mess. Took us the rest of the day to get them all back on the shelves!"

"What'd happened, d'you figure?"

"At first, Aunt Hazel thought it was kids from New Paris,

playing a prank. You know, they all think this place is haunted, and sometimes they come sneaking around just to show how big and brave they are. Huh! But then these other things started to happen."

"Other things like what?" Marco asked, taking the seat next to hers by the fireplace.

"That's what I wanted to tell you, boy."

Lily's long blonde hair had fallen forward again, and she batted it back angrily.

"Like, we went to a movie one Saturday afternoon, and it was so good I talked Aunt Hazel into seeing it over again. Funny? There was this one part where this man fell into this—anyhow, Marco, when we got back to Shady Hall, we saw this light in the attic, moving along from window to window."

"What did you do?"

"Let me tell you! We slipped into the house like a couple of Indians and locked ourselves in the living room and called Sheriff Gross on the telephone."

"Go on!" Marco urged.

Lily grabbed a yank of golden hair and swished it across her face.

"By the time old 'Wyatt Earp' came roaring up in his prowl car, with the siren going full blast, and came stomping into the house, twirling his ready six-gun, whatever-it-was had disappeared."

"How?"

Lily tossed the lock of hair back where it belonged.

"Who knows?"

"What else has happened?" the boy asked.

His cousin leaned forward, hugging herself with her strong, round arms. Her voice was hushed.

"Oh, listen, we've heard tapping and thumping—and

footsteps going up and down the hall at night. Up and down, up and down."

"You haven't seen anything?"

"Listen, boy, we're not *about* to unlock our doors to go snooping around."

"You lock your bedroom doors at night?" Marco asked in some surprise.

"Didn't you?" Lily was just as surprised as he. "Guess we should have told you last night, but we figured you'd have enough sense—"

"But you locked up downstairs before you went up to bed," the boy pointed out. "Don't you always do that?"

"Oh, sure. But there are so many doors and so many windows—and they've all got these rusty, old locks on them—so that if somebody wanted to get in, he wouldn't have much trouble."

"We'll have to take care of that," the boy told her.

"Anyway, how do we know it's somebody from outside?" his cousin asked. "Why not something from inside?"

"Oh, Lily, you don't believe there are ghosts in Shady Hall!"

She leaned forward, thrusting her hair back. Her voice was just above a whisper.

"Cousin Marco, I don't know what I believe about this place, but something awful funny is going on here. You just stay here a while and you'll know what I mean. Talk to Aunt Hazel—ask her about the letters."

"What letters?"

Lily's eyes bulged, and she pointed a shaky finger.

"Marco, look!"

The shawl in Miss Hazel's chair was moving. It trembled and shook, pushing out and pulling in, like a plot of ground about to erupt into a volcano.

"*Merr-ow!*"

The black head of Curious Cat stuck out from the edge of the shawl. His yellow eyes were in slits, like exclamation points without the points. He looked at the girl, he looked at the boy, and then he remarked, *"Merr-ow!"*

"He heard everything we said." Lily's voice was full of respect, mixed with a small amount of fear. "There's nothing that animal doesn't know. If he could only talk!"

"Maybe he can," Marco replied.

"What do you mean?"

"I'm going to see if I can get him to tell me what he knows."

"Brother! And *you* think *I'm* nuts. Okay, Marco, lotza luck. I'm going to help Aunt Hazel clean house. You two have you a nice chat, hear?"

The boy took the animal into his lap.

"Well, I don't think it'll be too hard, do you, Curious Cat?" he asked. "I talked to my tiger, asking him a mess of questions, and he answered me by signals like cocking his eyebrow for 'yes' and stretching his neck for 'no'. And tigers and cats are both in the same family—right?"

Curious Cat sat straight up in Marco's lap with his tail curled around him. He looked like one of those cat gods in ancient Egypt, all-wise, all-powerful. Dead serious, he watched the boy with his golden eyes.

"Right?" Marco repeated, stroking him under the chin. *"Merr-ow!"*

Curious Cat lay down in his lap, purring. He stretched out his left paw and laid it gently on the boy's right arm, as if to say, "I've got something to tell you."

Marco felt excitement swell in his chest. His voice was tight.

"Curious Cat, do you have something to tell me?"

"Merr-ow!"

"Does that mean 'yes'?"

"*Merr-ow!*"

"Does that mean 'no'?"

"*Merr-ow!*"

The boy took a deep breath. Patience, Marco. Patience!

"Does it mean *anything*?"

The animal looked up, regarding him solemnly, and silently.

Marco scratched him behind the ears.

"Curious Cat, are you going to talk to me?"

The animal shook his head so hard that Marco saw a golden swirl of eyes.

"*Rrrow!*"

"Curious Cat," the boy asked hopefully, "when you shake your head like that, do you mean 'no'?"

The animal raised his head high and yawned, giving Marco an excellent view of the roof of his mouth. Then the cat developed a sudden interest in his left paw. He gazed at it with his yellow eyes as if he had never seen that strange black thing before.

The boy gritted his teeth. "Now kindly pay attention to me," he urged.

Curious Cat decided to tidy up a bit. He gave his glossy coat a good going over, then began to work on his paws.

From somewhere else in Shady Hall there came a clatter and bang, as Lily and her great aunt did battle with the old house.

"Curious Cat," the boy told him, "I *must* know if you are trying to tell me something."

"*Merr-ow!*"

The animal rolled over on his back, stretching. He gazed up at Marco with golden, upside-down eyes.

"Curious Cat, are you listening to me?"

"*Merr-ow!*"

*The black head of Curious Cat stuck out from the edge of the shawl. He
looked ... then he remarked, "Merr-ow!"*

"I don't think you're trying to help me at all!"

Curious Cat twisted about, jumped down to the floor and sauntered out of the room, walking stiff-legged, remarking over his black shoulder, "*Merr-ow!*"

The boy gave his forehead the best slap of the day, so far.

"Marco, Marco," he told himself, "you've shot a whole entire morning and you haven't found out a single, solitary thing. You, boy, are a mess. I say again, a mess!"

Going out into the hall, he waited for the sounds of distant battle to die down for a bit, then called, "Miss Hazel, if it's okay with you, I'd like to go into New Paris and scout around"

"Be back before dark, Marco," she answered.

"Don't worry!"

As Marco was walking down the flagstones to the road, Tolliver burst through the opening in the bamboo and bounded toward him, puffing heavily. He sniffed the boy in a friendly fashion, accepted a pat on the head, and then bounded off in the direction of the cottage.

Eugene Gerard came jogging up. He sounded like Tolliver.

"Anybody here seen my dog?" he asked. "Greetings, Marco. Our morning jaunt," he explained. "It's good for Tolliver, and"—he took a deep breath—"it's good for me. Where you headed, man?"

"New Paris. Want to come?"

"Have a few pots I want to clean," Eugene Gerard said.

"That's right," Marco replied, remembering last night. "Need any help?"

"Naw. Listen pal, New Paris isn't exactly just around the corner. Why don't you take my bike?"

"Great!"

As Marco was pedaling down the driveway to the road, a fat kid about his age jumped out through the bamboo. He chanted in a sing-song voice:

"Shady Hall, Shady Hall!
Full o' gold an' ghosts an' all!"

He grabbed up a handful of mud and threw it at Marco. He missed by a yard. For a fat kid, he was able to run pretty fast. Marco could have ridden him down like a cavalryman after a foot soldier, but he let the kid go.

6

SCOUTING EXPEDITION

The clock in the courthouse tower (where they used to hang people in the old days) was striking twelve, as Marco came riding into the square on his trusty steed. The journey had given him a rare thirst. He parked the bike outside the Magnolia Drugstore and went in.

The drugstore smelled more of coffee and grilled cheese sandwiches than of drugs. Marco walked to the lunch counter in the rear.

A girl in a blue uniform, with "Edna" stitched on the pocket, wiped the counter in front of him with a damp rag.

"What'll you have, young man?"

"Coke, please."

"Large or small?"

"Large, of course," said a voice Marco recognized. "Can't you see he's a big spender?"

Tad Payne came slouching up to the counter and slumped onto a stool.

"Small, please," Marco told the girl, although he had planned to order a large one.

"Coffee, Edna," Mr. Payne ordered. His stool squealed as he turned to face the boy. He still hadn't shaved, and his hands were black with fresh grease.

"And how did we like our first night at Shady Hall?" he asked. "Did we see the *loup-garou?*"

Marco sipped his Coke, ignoring the second question and answering the first. "It was okay."

He glanced down at Tad Payne's feet. The mechanic was wearing heavy work boots, so it was hard to tell, but the feet seemed about the size of the footprint.

"Look at me, boy," Tad Payne ordered. "I don't like kids that won't look me in the eye. Expect you know why they call the place Shady Hall——'cause so many shady deals have been pulled there."

"Really?" Marco kept on sipping his Coke.

"Really." Tad Payne took a slurp of coffee. The mug was small and white in his big, grease-blackened hands. "And I'm not just talking about the old days neither," he added. "Know something, Edna? I never *have* been able to collect on that bill."

"Now, Tad," she chided him gently.

"It's a fact." He sat hunched forward, holding the mug with both hands. "I gave that car of Jim Danton's a complete overhaul—new battery, new plugs, new everything—had her running like a racer. 'Thanks, Tad. Great job.' But when it came time to settle up the bill, that was another story."

"Now, Tad."

Crack! went the black knuckles.

"I know, don't speak ill of the dead. But his sister could have paid me, couldn't she? He left her right well fixed, from all I hear. But I'll tell you something right now—the Dantons have never been known for their generosity."

Marco finished his Coke. He wanted to leave this unpleasant man, but he had come to town to get information, and maybe Mr. Payne could help him—even if the greasy mechanic wouldn't do it on purpose.

Caar-rack! went the knuckles of the other hand.

"No, sir," Tad Payne repeated, "the Dantons have never

been known for their generosity. Or," he added, "their loyalty to old friends."

"Now, Tad," Edna chided.

"All right, look at how they treated Antoine Boudier, after he was the family lawyer for so many years."

The stool squealed as if in great distress when Tad Payne whirled on it to face Marco again.

"Go see him. He'll tell you. He's right down the street, over J. C. Penney's. I call it shameful the way Jim Danton dropped Antoine. And I say Danton got just what he deserved when the Yankee lawyer messed up the whole deal. Antoine will tell you. Go see him. Right down the street."

Mr. Payne turned back to the waitress.

"Edna, remember when those precious azalea bushes of Hazel Danton's were dying? She had a professor with a big beard come out from the college to examine them.

" 'Miss Hazel,' " the prof says, " 'all these bushes need is for you to water them once in a while.' "

The mechanic slapped a dirty hand on the counter.

"Well, sir, right then Miss Hazel began to pray for rain!"

Tad Payne sounded like a truck starting up as he exploded with laughter. Edna gave a nervous giggle. The mechanic stared down at Marco.

"You're not laughing, boy."

"I don't see anything funny," Marco replied.

"This world of ours would be a right sad place if there weren't a few laughs now and then," Mr. Payne told him grimly. "My advice to you, boy, is to go back to New Orleans—the sooner, the better. And, as long as you're here, stay away from Henri Cassatt, the bridge tender. He don't like the Dantons or anything about them. It's for your own good I'm warning you. And another thing—steer clear of Big Green Swamp, you hear?"

"I hear."

"No telling how many nosey kids have gone in there and never come out."

As Marco was mounting Eugene Gerard's bike, he heard another explosion of laughter. Apparently, Tad Payne was trying to brighten up the world with another story about the Dantons.

The rusty old sign said:

ANTOINE BOUDIER
ATTORNEY AT LAW

The boy left the bike in the hallway, and climbed a flight of squeaky wooden stairs to the second floor. At the end of a long, dim, dusty, empty corridor was the law office of Antoine Boudier. Marco opened the door and entered a small, dim, dusty, empty waiting room. He was aware of a strange hush.

Out the dusty window, he could see the Civil War cannon aimed in his general direction; beyond it, the courthouse. The clock in the old hanging tower said 12:45. Dark clouds, like an endless herd of buffalo, were galloping over the courthouse from the south and the Gulf of Mexico.

As the boy gazed out, there was a sudden rattle, and a number of raindrops made neat, round, .45 caliber-sized holes in the dust on the windowpane. Not quite sure what to do next, Marco walked around the room.

A little white card on one gray wall next to a brown door said:

Please press buzzer and be seated.
Mr. Boudier will be with you shortly.

The boy pushed the green buzzer below the not-so-white card, and sat down in a tired, old chair, picking up a magazine that had been printed seven years before he had been born.

There was another rattle as a fresh flight of raindrops landed on the windowpane.

He could, Marco thought, watch the drops race down the glass, betting on one—that was always fun. Or he could read the eighteen-year-old magazine. *Or* he could do what he had come here for and get information.

The door next to the buzzer was not closed completely. The boy pushed it all the way open. He saw a room filled with books—law books—ten, twelve shelves of law books. At a desk facing him sat Antoine Boudier, Attorney at Law. A sign on the desk said exactly that.

"Mr. Boudier?" Marco asked softly, entering the room.

Antoine Boudier had a rather clean white handkerchief covering the top of his head. He sat very still. The light from the window gleamed on his spectacles, and he seemed to be staring straight into the boy's eyes.

"Mr. Boudier?" Marco repeated.

The lawyer made no answer. He appeared to be an unusually large man. His round head was quite close to the size of a basketball, his shoulders about the width of a grizzly bear's —and it wasn't padding because he was in his shirtsleeves. He sat silent, spectacles aglow, pink cheeks puffing out and in.

Of course, Antoine Boudier, Attorney at Law, was having himself a snooze.

For the third time, the boy asked, "Mr. Boudier?"

"Huh!"

The lawyer reached up his right hand, and pulled off the handkerchief from his pink, bald head. He put both pink hands on the arms of his chair and rose up, and up—past the fifth shelf of law books, the sixth, the seventh. He was the biggest, tallest, broadest, thickest human being Marco had ever seen.

"Antoine Boudier at your service," the lawyer said in a

voice that seemed rather small to be coming out of such a big man. His spectacles gleamed and he asked:

"What do *you* know for the good of your country?"

Marco had no quick answer for that question.

"*And*, if you don't mind my asking," Mr. Boudier went on, "what's the big idea of busting in on me like this?"

"I pressed the buzzer," the boy pointed out.

"That buzzer," the lawyer replied coldly, "has not worked in three years."

It appeared that Attorney Boudier had awakened a bit cranky from his nap.

He stretched out his arms—from one end of the room to the other—or so it seemed. Then carefully, very carefully, like a crane lowering a large, heavy, delicate piece of machinery into the hold of a freighter, Mr. Boudier sat back down. There was a hiss of air from the chair, and another from Mr. Boudier.

"Now then, young man," he said with something—just something—of a smile, "what can I do for you?"

"My name is Marco Fennerty, Junior," the boy told him. "I'm staying with Miss Hazel Danton at Shady Hall."

"Yes, I know."

"No kidding," the boy remarked in some surprise. "How did you know that?"

"The Spanish moss telegraph," the lawyer replied with something more of a smile. "Things get around right fast in a small town. To repeat, what can I do for you."

"I just saw Mr. Tad Payne," Marco replied, "and he said I should talk to you."

"Very well, Marco. You're talking—I'm listening."

Mr. Boudier made a pink tent of his fingers and watched the boy over it. The lawyer's hands, Marco thought, were small—but maybe they just seemed that way because the rest of him was so very, very big.

What about his feet? They were invisible under the desk.

"There has been some funny business at Shady Hall," the boy began. "I thought maybe you could give me some information."

The pink tent of fingers broke up into two pink fists, that plopped on the desk blotter as the lawyer leaned forward.

"Like what, if I may ask?"

"I don't know, sir," Marco admitted. "I'm just trying to figure out what's going on at Shady Hall."

Attorney Boudier smiled, really smiled this time. When a man with a face that size smiled, it was something to see. He commented, "The boy detective, investigating a case."

"I guess you could call it that," Marco agreed, somewhat embarrassed.

"I am well aware of your reputation, Marco," Attorney Boudier told him. "Oh, yes, we have a newspaper here—we're not *that* removed from civilization—and it carried the story about how you and that girl and the sleuth hound captured those crooks, and found the Confederate gold in Fort Beauregard. A fine job, if I may say so."

"Thank you, sir." Marco dropped his eyes, really embarrassed now.

"I'll be glad to answer any questions you might have," Mr. Boudier said, fingers returning to put up the tent. "But you must realize that I have to be careful to protect the interests of my client."

"Of course," Marco agreed. Then he asked, "Who's your client?"

"The late Jim Danton."

The boy's big eyes grew even bigger. "Really?"

Mr. Boudier carefully nodded his round, heavy head.

"Oh yes. I've been the Danton Family lawyer for a good many years. I drew up Jim's will. In it he named me executor, and administrator of the estate . . .

"In other words, Marco," he added, noticing the blank look on the boy's face, "I carry out the provisions of the will— I do what Jim wanted done, seeing that this person and that person gets certain money coming to them. It's very complicated."

"But I thought that lawyer in Washington had taken over, and Mr. Danton had made a will with him," Marco said.

Anger darkened the shade of pink in Mr. Boudier's basketball of a head.

"I wish I knew how that story got started," he muttered. He drew a deep breath. "Anyway, it's not true. Jim Danton hired a lawyer in Washington just to make the arrangements with the National Trust people about leaving them Shady Hall."

"But why did he have to hire another lawyer?" Marco asked. "Why didn't he just leave the house to the National Trust in his will?"

"It's not quite that simple. You don't just leave a house to the National Trust. First, they have to consider the property important enough to take over. Then the owner has to endow the property—leave a certain amount of money to help pay for the restoration and the upkeep. It's all very complicated," he repeated, "as anything *is* that deals with legal questions."

"The story is that the Washington guy messed everything up," the boy said.

Mr. Boudier's face grew darker yet, and his fists thudded on the blotter.

"More lies! There are laws in this state to take care of people who go around . . ."

He drew another deep breath.

"The 'Washington guy,' as you call him, is N. K. Allday,

a very able man, and highly respected in the profession. *Nobody* messed *anything* up."

The boy shook his head in confusion.

"Then what's the trouble, sir?" he asked. "Miss Hazel said that her brother didn't have as much money as he thought he had."

"Let me put it this way," Mr. Boudier explained. "Like so many people, Jim Danton lived as though he thought he would go on living forever. He did, however, have the good sense to make a will with the aid of legal counsel." The lawyer thrust a pink finger at his own chest.

"In this will," he went on, "the deceased left Shady Hall to the National Trust, along with an endowment of two hundred thousand dollars. He gave his sister Hazel the option —the choice—of staying in the house the rest of her life, or going somewhere else to live. If she chose to stay, Shady Hall would become the property of the National Trust upon her death. If she chose to leave, fourteen days thereafter the National Trust would take over. All right so far?"

"I guess so," Marco replied, not quite sure.

"The deceased further provided that any moneys—just say money—left over after the payment of certain bills, legal fees, and so forth and so on, would be the property of his sister. Are you still with me?"

"You mean Miss Hazel gets all the money that's left after all the bills are paid?" the boy asked.

"That's about the size of it," Mr. Boudier agreed. "There's just one problem."

"What's that?"

The lawyer reached out his right hand, took a pen from its holder on the desk, and began to doodle on a big yellow pad. Then he put down the pen and gazed at the boy.

"There's no money left," he said.

"How come?"

"How do I know how come?" the lawyer demanded. He picked up the pen once more, and drew a little house with smoke coming from the chimney. "There was no money in Jim's safety deposit box in the bank here. I checked and learned he had no accounts in any banks in New Orleans, New York, or Washington."

"Why did you check at those places?" the boy asked.

"Because, Marco," the lawyer answered with some irritation, "the deceased made frequent trips to those places the last few years of his life. AND," he warned, "don't ask me *why?* I didn't think it was any of my business."

Under the little house, the lawyer drew a big dollar sign.

"Mr. Boudier," Marco asked, "do you know how much money Jim Danton was planning to leave his sister?"

"He told me in a talk we had shortly before his death. The same amount as he left the National Trust—two hundred thousand dollars."

"Two hundred thousand dollars!"

"Correct," the lawyer replied, writing own: $200,000. Then he drew a line through the figure. "But, as I told you, this money has not turned up. And," he added with some more irritation, "don't ask me why, or where it might be—if indeed there *is* such a sum."

"Mr. Boudier," the boy asked, "where do you think Jim Danton got the money to, to—I can't think of the word."

"*Endow* Shady Hall for the National Trust? I don't know. I didn't think it was any of my business."

"I see," Marco replied. "Mr. Boudier, I guess you've heard the story that a pile of money is supposed to be hidden at Shady Hall."

"I've heard the story."

"Do you think it's true?"

"I don't know whether it's true or false," the lawyer answered. "All I know is *I* couldn't find any."

"You searched the house?" Marco asked softly.

The lawyer's spectacles gleamed as he gave the boy a steady gaze.

"*With* Hazel Danton at my side every step of the way," he added with some more irritation, and made another dollar sign on the yellow pad.

"If there *was* any money in the house," Marco asked, "would it belong to Miss Hazel?"

The lawyer drew what looked like a large dog in front of the little house.

"As the heir and legatee of the deceased, yes."

"What's a leg—?" the boy started to ask. "Never mind," he

added quickly.

"Marco," the lawyer told him, "I've lived right many years on this earth—just how many I'd rather not say—but I can sum up all I've learned in just seven words."

The attorney raised both fists, and as he spoke the words, he snapped up a pink finger:

"The (*snap*) wolf (*snap*) is (*snap*) always (*snap*) at (*snap*) the (*snap, snap*) door."

"The wolf?"

"In other words, we always have to worry about money problems."

"I see," the boy replied. "Mr. Boudier, what's Miss Hazel going to do now?"

"You'll have to ask her. Fortunately, she won't starve. She has a little money from a trust fund her father set up for her, but it's just barely enough for her to get by. At least, as long as she stays at Shady Hall, she has a roof over her head."

"But she doesn't want to stay at Shady Hall," Marco told him. "She wants to go to Florida and sit in the sun."

The lawyer shrugged his grizzly bear shoulders.

"She can't go anywhere without that other money. Of course, the National Trust is willing to put her up wherever she wants, but Miss Hazel is too proud. She'd consider that charity."

"She'll have to stay alone at Shady Hall the rest of her life?" Marco had a quiet shudder, thinking about Miss Hazel staying in the house that scared her so.

"I reckon."

"Mr. Boudier," the boy said, "there's just one more question."

"Just one more? Good!" the lawyer stuck the pen firmly back in its holder.

"You told me that Jim Danton said in his will that Miss

Hazel would get all the money left over after the bills and legal fees and all were paid."

"Yes?" The lawyer was watching him closely from behind his spectacles.

The boy took a deep breath. "I was just wondering. . . ."

The pink face darkened considerably, and the hands on the desk became fists.

"You were just wondering," the lawyer growled, standing up, and up—and up—"if my fee might be in the neighborhood of two hundred thousand dollars—is that it?"

Marco took another deep breath. "Yes, sir."

"Well it isn't! Both my fee and what Mr. Allday charged are quite fair—*quite* fair—but just how much we charged, young man, is none of your business!"

The attorney slammed his fist down on the blotter so hard that the frightened pen jumped out of its holder, scrambled across the desk, and dropped to the floor.

"I'll get it!" the boy exclaimed. Running around to the lawyer's side of the desk, he knelt on the floor.

"What do you think you're doing down there?" the man demanded from his great height, trying to see the boy over his impressive stomach.

Mr. Boudier had taken off his shoes—probably for his nap—and now was in his stocking feet. Antoine Boudier, Attorney at Law, had a hole in the sock of his left foot; and his pink big toe was sticking out! His feet (and big toe) looked small in comparison to the rest of him, but Marco figured they were about the size of the footprint.

"Get up there, and get out of here!" the lawyer thundered.

"Yes, sir," the boy replied. "Your pen, sir," he went on, sticking it back in the holder. "Good-by, sir," he added, making his legs walk, when they wanted to run, out of the room.

7

THE SHERIFF
OF NAPOLEON PARISH

Marco pedalled past the Civil War cannon and the steady iron gaze of the Confederate Memorial, then parked Eugene Gerard's bike by the front entrance to the courthouse. From the outside, the old brick building did not look like a very happy place. The inside seemed even unhappier.

The boy felt as though he were smack in the middle of a pyramid. The long, dark corridor smelled of years and years of sadness, washed down with strong, soapy water. At the end of the hall, by a flight of stairs, a sign said:

NAPOLEON PARISH
SHERIFF'S OFFICE

An arrow pointed up the stairs.

Marco climbed the worn marble steps, pulling himself along by a railing that looked as though it had come off *Old Ironsides* after one of her better sea battles. At the top of the staircase he walked down another corridor, past doors that said, "WATER BOARD," "HEALTH DEPARTMENT," and "REGISTRAR OF VOTERS" to a door that said, "SHERIFF'S OFFICE."

He knocked. From inside there was a sudden burst of typing, like a submachine gun getting off fifty rounds rapid fire.

"Come in," a man's voice ordered.

Marco entered a small office. It was just about filled by filing cabinets, a framed photograph of the President of the United States, and a desk, behind which sat a young man in a snappy uniform consisting of dark blue trousers and a white shirt, with a silver deputy sheriff's badge on his chest. Across one shoulder was a patch that said, "NAPOLEON PARISH SHERIFF'S DEPARTMENT." In case you missed that, there was a second patch on the other shoulder that said the same thing.

"What's your's lad?" the deputy sheriff asked. "Stolen bicycle?" Then he added, "Hey, you're not from around here."

"No, sir," Marco admitted. "But I'd like to see the sheriff."

"Business or pleasure?"

"Business."

The deputy gave another fifty-round burst of the typewriter, then said, "We're right busy, but I'll see what I can do."

He arose and swaggered to an inner door, hand on his gun. "Sheriff, kid here claims he wants to see you on business."

"Okay, Jasper, send him in."

"Don't stay too long," the deputy whispered as the boy passed him.

Sheriff Sam Y. Gross arose and came around from behind his desk, a big brown hand out. He was tall and lean, as sheriffs are supposed to be. He wore trim blue pants and a white shirt with gold stars on the shoulder, and a gold sheriff's badge on the chest. A pair of black cowboy boots completed his sharp-looking uniform.

"Howdy, pardner," he greeted the boy. "What can I do for you?"

The sheriff had a heavy brown handlebar mustache that seemed to pull his face down. His shaggy eyebrows were like two smaller mustaches. Marco thought he must have spent much of his life outdoors, he was so deeply tanned. There were lines across his forehead, and at the outer corner of each eye. His shirt collar was unbuttoned, showing his brown lined neck.

Marco wondered if he could tell how old the law man was by the number of lines in his neck, the way you could the age of a tree by counting its rings. Judging from the lines, Sheriff Gross was about a hundred and fifty years old.

Around his slim waist was a cartridge belt from which hung a huge nickel-plated revolver. From the other side dangled a pair of brass handcuffs that jingled as he walked.

"I won't be long, Sheriff," the boy promised as they shook hands. "The deputy said y'all were right busy."

"Election year," the law man explained.

From the next room the typing sounded like a gun battle.

"My name is—" the boy began.

"Marco Fennerty," the sheriff finished the sentence.

"Junior," the boy added, his face burning. It was nice to be known, but it was embarrassing, too.

"Recognized you from the picture in the paper," the law man told him. "Wish I'd been on that case."

"I'm on another one now," the boy told him, "along with my Cousin Lily and my friend Eugene Gerard. I'd like to talk to you about it."

The sheriff motioned his visitor to a chair, sitting down at his desk by an American flag, and under a framed photograph of Wyatt Earp. The law man pulled on his handlebar mustache.

"Shoot, pard."

Quickly Marco told all that had happened since he had arrived in town and then at Shady Hall yesterday evening, and his conversations with Tad Payne and Antoine Boudier this morning. As he talked, wind moaned outside and rain spattered on the window. The sheriff listened to the boy intently, pulling first one handle of his mustache, then the other.

"Too bad about that footprint," he remarked.

"It sure is," the boy agreed. "Sheriff, people keep talking about Henri Cassatt, the bridge tender. They say he was mad at Jim Danton for some reason."

"I can't confirm that," the law man replied. "Confirm it or deny it. It's true enough that Henri did not attend Jim's funeral—about the only one in New Paris who didn't."

"Was Tad Payne there?" the boy asked.

"He sure was, carrying on like it was *his* brother getting planted."

"Maybe Mr. Payne thought that Miss Hazel would pay his repair bill if he showed up at the funeral," Marco suggested.

"Maybe. I can't confirm that or deny it."

Gunfire—real gunfire—sputtered in the room. The sounds came from a box on Sheriff Gross's desk, which the boy saw now was a small television set. The sheriff, Marco thought, must have been watching a movie, and turned the sound down when the deputy told him he had a visitor.

Noticing the boy's eyes, the law man moved the set around so they both could see the screen.

"This is a good part," he said, turning up the volume.

A mess of horsemen were galloping along a dirt road, firing back at a bigger mess of horsemen that were chasing them, guns ablaze.

"Who're the good guys and who're the bad guys?" Marco asked.

Suddenly, the screen went black. Then the word "BULLETIN" appeared, and then a deep voice announced:

"We interrupt this program to bring you a special report from our news room. . . ."

The sheriff motioned Marco to sit down...by an American flag and under a photograph of Wyatt Earp.

The next scene was the news room, noisy with teletype machines trying to show how busy they were. A man in a business suit and tie, with an earphone snapped on one ear, sat before a microphone. He gave a brief nod to somebody and announced:

"Hurricane Inez, acting anything but lady like, has changed course again and is now headed for the southwest Louisiana coast. Inez, packing winds of ninety miles an hour, is expected to hit in the vicinity of New Paris, Louisiana, about midnight tonight."

"Hey now!" the law man exclaimed.

"*Gungah!*" Marco agreed.

"Residents in low-lying areas are warned to evacuate to higher ground," the announcer went on. "The Red Cross and National Guard are standing by, ready to move in if needed. Stay tuned to this station, 'Pride of the Southland,' for further details. We now return you to the feature movie, 'Riders of Cactus Gulch.'"

Sheriff Gross turned off the set, telling the boy, "Saddle up. I'll drive you home."

"But you'll miss the movie."

"Seen it three times," the law man replied, clamping on his hat. "Come on, pard. Saddle up!"

The racing dark clouds seemed to be no more than ten feet above the courthouse tower. The rain smelled of fish and the sea. It same in bunches, fleeing from the wind. By the time Sheriff Gross and Marco had put the bike in the trunk of the patrol car, the law man's shirt didn't look so sharp. But he probably had another fresh one at home.

"Oh, I hope it hits here!" the boy exclaimed.

"Bet you do," Sheriff Gross replied. "And you know something, pard? I kind of hope so myself. Time we had a little excitement in this place." He grinned and winked at the boy.

"Sheriff, we were talking about Henri Cassatt," Marco reminded him as they drove away from the square. "Do you know any other reason why people would think he was mad at Jim Danton?"

"This town of New Paris is a small one, as you might have noticed," the law man replied, guiding the patrol car around a bend in the road. "Small in more ways than one. People here will talk about anything. But right much was made of the fact that Henri Cassatt was the last person to see Jim Danton alive."

"How come?"

"He opened the bridge for him that day, as he always did. Jim sailed past down the bayou to Vermilion Bay, where he had his accident."

"That's right!" the boy told him. "The paper said there was a mystery about his death, or something like that."

"No mystery," Sheriff Gross answered. "A sharp wind came up, the boom swung around and hit Jim in the back of the head, knocking him overboard. Happens all the time. Unfortunately, Jim wasn't wearing a life preserver, as ordered by law."

"Mr. Danton was by himself in the boat?" Marco asked.

"Jim always sailed alone."

"Are you guessing about the wind making the boom knock him overboard?"

"Only way it could have happened, pard. Jules Latrobe, a fishing boat operator, was out in the bay at the time, in his own vessel. He came up, saw the empty boat wallowing in the waves and the boom swinging free, and towed the boat back in. Four days later, Jim's body washed up on the beach."

The boy ran his fingers through his shaggy, wet hair.

"I guess someone checked the body," Marco said.

"Right, pard. The coroner examined the remains, as he does any death thought to be from other than natural causes."

"Did he find any marks?"

The sheriff nodded. "The usual scratches from rubbing against marsh grass and oyster shells, and a bruise on the back of the head—such as a boom might make swinging around with the wind."

"Or a club might make?" Marco asked softly.

Sheriff Gross gave the boy a sharp glance.

"Yup, the same sort of bruise could have been made by a club," he agreed. "Your theory is that someone slipped up behind Jim and conked him one."

"I was just wondering," the boy said.

"And, with Jim knocked out, his boat sails itself around all the twists and turns of Bayou Terror till it gets to Vermilion Bay. Then Jim comes to, staggers to his feet, still groggy, loses his balance and falls overboard, drowning—that the idea?"

"I was just wondering," the boy repeated.

"Interesting theory, pard. It's possible, about as possible as this old prowl car getting itself lightning-struck. It's true, of course, that there was no witness to Jim's death and we have only circumstantial evidence to go on. But circumstantial evidence stands up in a court of law. At the inquest, the coroner's jury brought in a verdict that 'the deceased met his death by accidental drowning, having been knocked overboard by the swinging boom of his sailboat, the wind being gusty.' Pard, I've served eight straight terms as sheriff of Napoleon Parish— up for reelection this November coming—and I'll stake my reputation on it: the verdict of the coroner's jury is good enough for me."

"Yes, sir," Marco replied. "Then just because Henri

Cassatt was the last man to see Jim Danton alive, that's no reason to think he had anything to do with Mr. Danton's death."

"My opinion exactly, pard," the law man agreed. "Only try to tell that to these people. Somebody without enough to do has started a raft of rumors, and other folks are only too happy to keep passing them around."

The patrol car skidded like a boat in a sudden gust of wind. The daylight had turned green, and the windshield was a rainy blur in spite of the steady efforts of the wipers.

"Sheriff, do you think the same guy started the rumor about Shady Hall being haunted?" Marco asked.

"I've heard that all my life. And my daddy heard it when he was a kid."

"What about the one about a pile of money being hidden there?" the boy asked.

"Same thing. These stories *will* grow up about an old house, and there's nothing you can do to stop them."

The patrol car came to a big branch lying across the road. The law man and Marco jumped out and dragged it to the side, getting thoroughly drenched in the process.

"Sheriff, what kind of a guy is Henri Cassatt?" the boy asked when they were back in the car.

"He's a Cajun."

Marco glanced at the brown, lined face of the law man, waiting for him to go on.

"Henri is old and a mite strange, and has an awful temper, but I like him fine," the sheriff said. "Give you an idea what I mean. I was out on a holdup other side of Bayou Terror one night, got back about nine. Stopped at the bridge to say howdy. Henri lives in a little shack, he built himself right next to the bridge.

"We were having us a cup of coffee when somebody calls

from the bayou. It's Jim Danton, out for a moonlight sail, and he wants Henri to open the bridge so he can get by.

"This is a swing bridge, and Henri has to operate it with just his muscle. He goes out, muttering about people that go sailing when they should be in bed. But he opens the bridge and Jim sails on by.

"Henri and I got to talking and didn't notice the time. Then, about eleven, here comes Jim Danton back up the bayou, calling for the bridge to be opened again. I mean Ole Henri blew up. He goes storming off, saying, 'I'm gonna cuss that man out.'

"He opens the bridge. Jim comes by and says with a big grin, 'Thanks, Henri. Good night!'

"Ole Henri grins right back and says, 'Good night, Jim!'

"I says, 'Thought you were gonna cuss him out.'

"Ole Henri gives me this look and says, 'He knew what I was thinking.' "

Marco joined the sheriff in a laugh. The tires made a crunching sound. They had come to the shell road. Wind whipped the Spanish moss, hanging like torn gray banners from the branches overhead.

A thought was somewhere in the back of the boy's mind, but he couldn't get hold of it, like a fugitive bar of soap in the bathtub. He had forgotten to do something—what? Of course! He had forgotten to ask Antoine Boudier, Attorney at Law, if it was true that Jim Danton hadn't left Henri Cassatt any money in his will.

Whack! Drops of water flew as Marco slapped himself on the forehead.

"What's the trouble, pard?"

"I guess you heard the story that Mr. Cassatt is supposed to be mad because Jim Danton didn't leave him any money?" the boy asked.

"I've heard the story. I can't confirm or deny it. Maybe Jim did leave Henri something and maybe he didn't. Maybe Henri is mad and maybe he isn't. But Antoine Boudier is Jim's lawyer. He can tell you what's in the will."

"I know. I forgot to ask him about that," the boy replied. "Sheriff, what kind of a person was Jim Danton?"

The law man guided the patrol car around one bend, then another. The over-worked windshield wipers cleared the glass with each stroke, only to have the rain blur it the next second.

"I knew Jim Danton since we were in first grade together," the sheriff answered. "But I never really *knew* him, if you get my meaning."

"I'm not sure."

"Jim was always quiet, even when he was a kid. You never knew what he was thinking—because he wouldn't tell you. Dreamy type. Sit for hours and not say a word. He was a great one for drawing, used to have pictures all over his books and papers. All the teachers said he should go to art school."

"Did he?"

"He studied art in France for years. Then he came back to New Paris, just before World War Two broke out. 'Hi, Sam,' he says, just as if he'd been gone for a week end. Then he holed up in Shady Hall and hardly ever came out, except to go sailing—usually at night—or to go off on one of his trips."

"Where was Miss Hazel then?" Marco asked.

"Shady Hall. Jim came home and found her living there alone, with the house falling down around her ears. Then Jim and Miss Hazel lived there together for more than thirty years—until his accident."

Sheriff Gross gave the boy a quick glance. "But you know, pard, Miss Hazel could fill you in on right much of this."

"I know," Marco agreed. "To tell the truth, I haven't had much chance to talk to her yet. But there must be a mess of stuff, you know that she probably doesn't, like about Henri Cassatt and what the people in town are saying."

The sheriff reached out a long arm of the law and clapped the boy on the shoulder.

"Well, pard, I'll help you all I can. But you know what folks around here are saying is mostly gossip. And that wouldn't stand up in court."

"Yes, sir, but I think maybe the gossip is an important part of this case," Marco replied.

"You might be right there. I'll tell you now, folks here did not approve of Jim traipsing around Europe, and leaving Miss Hazel alone—no, sir, not a bit. They also did not approve of him running off to New York and Washington, spending money they reckoned he couldn't afford. Of course, I say that was Jim's business and none of theirs. But they say different."

"Maybe he went up there to sell his paintings," the boy suggested.

"I doubt it, pard, I really do. It's true Jim came back from Europe with a raft of paintings. I never saw any myself, but some of the town ladies paid Shady Hall a visit shortly after he returned, and Miss Hazel showed them what Jim had done over there. She was right proud of those paintings, I understand, but the ladies said afterward that none of them were of much account."

"How would they know?" Marco asked.

"True," the sheriff agreed. "None of the ladies were art experts, as far as I know. The whole thing is, there's no pleasing the people of New Paris, as far as Shady Hall and the Dantons are concerned."

"I see."

"Jim Danton was secretive—not sneaky, mind—*secretive*. Folks here want to know what's going on all the time, but with Jim Danton, mum was always the word."

The patrol car swerved to the right, and Marco saw Bayou Terrebonne. Raindrops made thousands of tiny fountains in the green water, thousands more appearing as quickly as the others disappeared. Shady Hall was only a few minutes away, and there was still so much he wanted to know.

"Sheriff," the boy asked, "what do you think all this funny business at Shady Hall means?"

Thoughtfully, the law man drove in silence along the twisting bayou. . . . Finally he answered, "Shady Hall is an old house, and an old house makes strange noises. On the other hand, it doesn't howl, or show mysterious lights, or throw all the books in the study on the floor—not by itself it doesn't."

"I'm with you," Marco told him.

"It also doesn't write letters."

"Letters?" the boy repeated. "Oh, my Cousin Lily said something about that!"

"Ask Miss Hazel to show them to you," the law man told him. "She should have quite a collection by now. Up until a short time ago, I thought they were being written by a crank."

Marco nodded. He understood.

"Now," the sheriff added, "I'm not so sure."

The boy glanced at him. He did not understand.

Ahead, the gables of Shady Hall appeared over the hedge of bamboo, that swayed and rattled and crashed in the wind. For the moment, the rain had stopped; Shady Hall loomed huge and grim in the weird green light.

Suddenly, the patrol car radio sputtered. A scratchy, nervous voice exclaimed, "Headquarters calling Car One. Car One, come in, please!"

The tires crunched to a halt at the Danton driveway. The sheriff picked up the microphone from the dashboard and said, "Sheriff Gross."

"Car One, Deputy Hornbrook calling."

The law man glanced at Marco, shrugging his shoulders. "I know that, Jasper. What's the trouble?"

"Sheriff, refugees are coming in here like it's the Parish Fair! What'll I do with 'em?"

"Put 'em in the schoolhouse, Jasper," the law man told him briskly. "Then, when that's filled up, put 'em in the courthouse."

"Roger. Phone's ringing off the wall, Sheriff. Reckon you might be coming by this way any time soon?"

"On my way, Jasper. Ten-four?"

"Roger and out—only hurry!"

"Duty calls," the law man told Marco. "Reckon you can make it up to the house on your own?"

"I reckon."

The sheriff helped the boy drag the bike out of the back of the patrol car, then closed the trunk. The click sounded like a giant handcuff snapping shut.

"Pard," the law man said, "we're dealing with a right intelligent criminal here. Right desperate. Right dangerous. I didn't think so before, but I think so now. Expect I'll have my hands full in the parish tonight. Reckon you can hold down matters at Shady Hall?"

"I reckon."

"I'll check back with you if I can," Sheriff Gross told him. "No telling what might come up tonight. I'll see you, pard."

"See you, Sheriff," the boy replied.

The patrol car moved off with a whirling blue flash from its signal light and a howl from the siren.

8

LETTERS FROM ALL OVER

Before he started up the driveway, Marco checked the mailbox on its wooden stand by the road. There was something for Lily, a few things for Miss Hazel, and nothing for himself. He hadn't expected anything, but it was always nice to get mail.

An old automobile was parked in the driveway by the Danton car.

The boy dried off the bike thoroughly and returned it to Eugene Gerard. Then he hurried over to Shady Hall, entering through the kitchen. Miss Danton was having a cup of coffee there with a man who looked familiar.

"Marco," she said, "you remember Dr. Slade."

"Oh, of course. Hi, Dr. Slade."

"Good afternoon, Marco." The man extended his right hand. He was a rather small person but he had large hands, to go along with his big white teeth. His hair was dark brown. He had more than he really needed, and it was having its own way with his small head.

"That was nice of you to give Marco a ride yesterday evening," Miss Hazel told tim.

"What are friends for?" Dr. Slade asked. "I have to be going, Miss Danton," he went on. "I just came by to drop off this medicine. You *must* get some sleep. Two tablespoons in a glass of warm water at bedtime. You'll like this. It tastes just like strawberry syrup." He rose from the table and Marco noted that he had large feet, too.

"I hate strawberry syrup," his patient snapped.

"I love it," Lily told him, coming in from the other room.

Dr. Slade grinned at the girl and boy.

"Lily, Marco," he said, "I'm appointing y'all to see that she takes this tonight. If she doesn't get some sleep, she's going to have a nervous breakdown for sure."

He pulled on his raincoat and clapped a big hat on his small head.

"I'm off. The LaBlancs are worse, or think they are. Are y'all planning to stay here tonight or move to higher ground?"

"Stay here," Miss Hazel, Lily, and Marco answered together.

"If you need me for any reason, call me—no matter what time of night." The doctor handed Hazel Danton a business card. "Wait, that's my old number."

He reached his big right hand into his coat pocket, and brought out a gold pen. Crossing out the printed phone number, he wrote down another.

"Remember—anytime. If I'm not out on a call, I'll come running."

"Thank you, Doctor," Miss Hazel replied.

"What are friends for?" he asked. "I'm off!"

"Oh, I almost forgot," Marco said when Dr. Slade's car had gone crunching down the driveway. He gave Lily her mail, and started to give Miss Hazel hers. The latter reached out a hand, then jerked it back as though the boy had been offering her a snake. She gasped as if bitten and her face was paler than ever.

"Another one," she breathed.

"Another what?" Marco asked.

"Another of those letters," Lily said in a small voice.

Miss Hazel accepted the rest of the mail, muttering, "Bills." Then she told the boy, "Read the letter."

Marco tore the envelope open. On a single sheet of white paper, in the middle of the page, one short sentence was written:

Get out of that house

"*Gungah!*" the boy exclaimed. "It says—"

"Never mind," Miss Hazel told him. "I don't want to hear."

"Show him the others, Aunt Hazel," Lily urged.

"What's the good?" Miss Danton asked, her haunted eyes big and dark in her white face.

"Please, Aunt Hazel. Maybe he can figure something out from them."

Without another word, Miss Hazel walked into the study.

"*Merr-ow!*"

Curious Cat was curled up on Miss Danton's favorite chair. He watched the three people for a moment, then closed his golden eyes and made a black ball of himself, covering his black face with his paws, adding, "*Rrrow!*"

The Mistress of Shady Hall moved over to the desk, as if she had to force herself every step of the way. She paused in front of the desk, took a deep breath, then jerked the top open.

The inside was packed with letters, some of which popped out, fluttering to the floor.

"*Gungah!*"

"Read a few—but not out loud," Miss Hazel told him, her nervous eyes snapping around the room, looking everywhere but at the letters, many of which were still unopened.

The boy took a sheet of paper out of an envelope. The

sentence was exactly the same as the one in today's letter. Still another repeated the message. On a third was written:

That house is cursed

Marco, crouching on the floor, gazed up from the letters to Miss Danton and his cousin. Miss Hazel's eyes were still flitting nervously around the room. Lily was watching him with an eager smile, waiting for Detective Fennerty to say something brilliant.

"Sheriff Gross told me he used to think a cranky guy wrote these letters," the boy remarked.

"A cranky guy?" Miss Hazel asked, confused. "Oh, you mean a *crank*. There's quite a difference, Marco. A crank is someone who is trying to cause trouble just to cause trouble, a person who doesn't have his good sense."

Marco's face felt as if it had a bad sunburn. "Anyway, the sheriff says he's not so sure now," he added lamely.

"Every letter I've opened has either the one message or the other," Miss Hazel told him. "But they can't be sent by just one person. Look at the postmarks. They come from all over the country."

The boy checked a dozen or so envelopes. All were addressed:

The Dantons
Shady Hall
New Paris,
Louisiana

It was true that the letters seemed to come from all over the United States. One was postmarked "St. Louis, Missouri"; another "Memphis, Tennessee"; a third "Cincinnati, Ohio";

"Read a few — but not out loud," Miss Hazel told Marco, her nervous eyes
snapping around the room.

a fourth "Omaha, Nebraska"; a fifth "Minneapolis, Minnesota."

Both Lily and her great-aunt were now watching the boy. "*Merr-ow!*" So was Curious Cat.

"Marco, what do you think it all means!" Lily asked.

The boy scooped up the letters from the floor, stuck them back in the desk, and pulled down the top.

"I don't know," he admitted. "I'll have to work on it."

"*A cranky guy,*" Lily said, almost to herself. "Brother!"

The boy gave her a look. She grabbed a yank of yellow hair and threw it like a curtain over her face.

Marco turned to the owner of Shady Hall. "Miss Hazel, what do *you* think about these letters?" he asked. "You must have some idea."

Miss Hazel's nervous green eyes met the boy's steady brown eyes for a moment.

"I don't know, Marco." She gave a shudder. Then she straightened herself and forced a smile. "Who's for lunch?"

"Lunch!" Lily exclaimed.

"*Merr-ow!*"

Curious Cat led the way to the kitchen.

The rain came and went—came and went—all afternoon, as if having an angry argument with the old house. It would go off for a while, then return as though it had just thought of something else to say.

During one slack period, Miss Hazel took Marco out to show him the Union shell stuck in the chimney. Lily had seen it before, but came along anyway. Curious Cat, for once, was not interested and stayed stretched out under the kitchen stove, taking an after-lunch nap.

Outside, torn dark clouds were roaring overhead. Squadrons of gulls and other sea birds were flying up from the stormy south, complaining bitterly about having been forced to leave home. Slowly, Bayou Terrebonne was rising in its banks.

"You see, Marco," Miss Hazel told him, pointing down the bayou, "the Yankee gunboat came around that bend and opened fire on our troops stationed in Shady Hall. Most of the shells missed, but one hit the chimney up there."

"*Gungah!*" the boy exclaimed. "If it had gone off, it probably would have blown the whole house up!"

"Over here is the family graveyard," Miss Hazel continued, walking to a small plot of ground in which there were a number of flat gray stones. On most of them was carved just a name, along with the years of birth and death. One, however, caught Marco's eye. The neat letters cut into the stone said:

WILLIARD DANTON
1838-1858
Killed in a Duel
With Roy Knee

"Who was Roy Knee?" Marco asked.

"Huh-huh-huh-huh!"

Tolliver came bounding up from the bayou, politely sniffed all three of them in turn, then bounded off again. A few seconds later, Eugene Gerard appeared.

"Anybody here seen my dog?" he asked.

Rain hit them as they stood there in the little graveyard, drumming like volleys of Minié balle against the side of the house. Tolliver came bounding back and greeted his master effusively.

"Let's get in," Miss Hazel exclaimed. "Eugene Gerard, you and Tolliver come along, too!"

Shady Hall echoed with the racket of hammering, as Marco and Eugene Gerard worked their way from door to door, and window to window on the first floor, making certain that all were secure. Locks and bolts that were loose, they screwed or nailed tight. Others that were broken, they repaired or replaced from a big tool box located on the enclosed back porch.

Tolliver followed right along behind them, chuckling to himself in the way he had. Curious Cat watched them for a while, but the noise made him nervous, and he went off somewhere to hide.

Lily helped, too. She banged three nails, her thumb, and a forefinger. Her great-aunt came around once in a while to tell all the laborers "Careful now. Have some more cocoa."

"Whew!" Eugene Gerard remarked as Marco and he were returning the hammer and other gear to the toolbox. "That was *work*. But nobody that isn't welcome is getting in this house again."

Marco picked up a bucket from a corner of the porch.

"Hey, Eugene Gerard," he said, "what do you think about fixing us a little prowler trap?"

"You mean, fill the bucket with water and rig it so, when he opens the porch gate, he gets soaked? I think it's a great idea."

"I'll fill the bucket."

When Marco returned from the kitchen, lugging the heavy, sloshy bucket his friend had a long two-by-four that he was tying loosely to the gate with a piece of wire. Eugene Gerard then opened the stepladder, that was leaning against the lattice, and climbed to the porch ceiling with the bucket.

Marco stuck the two-by-four under the bucket. Too short, much *too* short. When the older boy dragged out a wooden box from another corner, however, and piled a couple of bricks on top of it, they all made a snug fit. At last, the bucket stood on its stand, waiting for the prowler.

"It'll hold," Eugene Gerard said. "The house will protect it from the wind until our friend pulls the gate open. Then *ker-bloom!* School's out.

"But you know something, Marco," he added as he climbed down the stepladder, "I was just thinking—"

"I was just thinking the same thing," his friend agreed. "If the prowler comes in from a hard rain tonight, a bucket of water isn't going to make much of an impression."

"Hey, man," Eugene Gerard exclaimed, "how about this frying pan? Seems to me we could use it some way."

He took down a big rusty skillet from the wall. It looked as though the Yankees had forgotten it when they had moved out at the end of the War Between the States—or maybe they had left it on purpose.

"Yeah, man," Marco replied, "we could rest it on top of that cupboard and tie it to the handle of the bucket—"

"So when somebody opens the gate the frying pan comes down, too," Eugene Gerard went on, climbing back up the stepladder with the skillet. "It should make a pretty nice noise when it hits the floor."

"You know," Marco said, "this porch is just full of stuff for a prowler trap. I feel like Robinson Crusoe on the desert island with a whole ship filled with things to play around with."

His friend gazed down at him from the stepladder. "Only I'm not your Man Friday, man."

"Course not," Marco agreed quickly. "Hey, how about this pot? Can't we use it someway?"

He held out an old iron vessel he had found in the cupboard.

"Sure, hand it up. We can tie it to the frying pan, so if

that doesn't wake everyone up when it hits the floor, the pot *will*."

"But wouldn't it be better if we put something in the pot, like marbles? . . ." Marco opened the toolbox, searching. "Or . . . tacks?"

"Yeah, he'll do some high stepping, if he comes back in his bare feet again!"

"Huh-huh-huh-huh!" Tolliver chuckled.

Marco took a double handful of tacks from the drawer in the toolbox, dropped them, rattling in the pot, and handed the whole business up. Eugene Gerard set the pot down on top of the cupboard and carefully wired the handle to the skillet.

"Hey, you guys, how about this can of paint?"

The two boys and Tolliver glanced around. Lily had returned from soaking her injured hand. She held up a small can of bright red paint.

"If some splashed on the prowler, wouldn't that be a good idea?" she asked.

"Yeah!" Eugene Gerard agreed. "Then maybe we could track him down later, even if he got away. Hand it up."

Marco pried open the can with a screwdriver and passed the paint on up the ladder. His friend wired the can to the handle of the pot.

"Now then," Eugene Gerard told the others as he folded up the stepladder, and gave their prowler trap a final check, "we're all set."

The boys, the girl, and the dog trooped back into the house. Marco locked and bolted the door behind them.

"I'll see you people later," Eugene Gerard said at the door of the study. "Come on, Tolliver!"

The rain had come rushing back with another strong argument. Eugene Gerard and his dog were soaked by the time they reached the cottage.

"Marco," Lily exclaimed, "look!"

The bayou had risen almost to the top of its banks, but that was not what she meant. A number of *V*s had appeared on the dimpled surface of the water, moving up the bayou.

"Snakes," the boy told her. "Heading for higher ground."

"Look there! That's no snake!"

A much bigger *V* had come into view. Then they saw a long, low, black shape, like a floating log—and a single, glinting eye.

"Alligator," Marco told her.

Along the far bank, muskrats and water rats were scurrying northward. They were followed by a shaggy, gray animal, about the size of a cocker spaniel, that came shambling along as if it didn't see too well, giving a loud wail.

"Nutria," Marco said.

"Close the door," Lily told him. "And lock it."

"Where's Miss Hazel?"

"Laying down—lying down," she corrected herself, taking a handful of blonde hair and tossing it over her shoulder.

"Listen, Cousin Marco, I want to know. *What's going on here?*"

They sat before the fireplace, as they had that morning. Wind passing over the chimney sounded as if a giant had blown across the mouth of a very large bottle. Then there came another noise, so soft that Marco was not sure he had heard it, a sound that was somehow familiar, but which he could not identify at the moment.

"Come on, boy," Lily told him.

"Well, I think somebody is pulling a mess of tricks, trying to scare your aunt out of Shady Hall."

"Great-aunt," Lily corrected. "Why?"

"I guess because whoever-it-is wants to be alone so he can

search the house without anyone bothering him."

"For the money!"

"That's *supposed* to be hidden here," the boy added.

"Do you think there *is* any?"

"I don't know. It appears that *somebody* thinks so."

"Who? Come on, Marco, don't hold out on me."

The boy shook his head. "I don't know, Lily."

"Honest Injun?"

"Honest Injun."

"Who do you think it might be? *Whom?*" she corrected herself.

"I don't know. It must be somebody from around here."

"But what about those letters from all over the country?"

"I haven't figured that out yet. I think Miss Hazel has an idea, but she doesn't want to talk about it for some reason. I still think the guy that's causing all the trouble is from New Paris. He must have heard the gossip about the pile of money being hidden in Shady Hall. And I think that now he's in a big hurry to get Miss Hazel out of here."

"What's the hurry?"

"If there *is* money hidden in Shady Hall—and I can't confirm or deny that—the workmen are bound to find it when they start fixing up the place for the National Trust."

That pesky lock of hair had slipped down over Lily's face again. She tossed it back where it had come from.

"What's your plan?"

"Well, I'm going to see Henri Cassatt, the bridge tender, tomorrow," the boy told her. "Want to come along?"

"You bet!"

"He might be dangerous."

"Huh!"

Outside, the wind moaned and rain drilled against the house. Then, from within Shady Hall, came that noise Marco had heard before. It sounded as if it came from far away, slipping from room to room, and down the long, dim corridors—a long, low sigh.

The boy glanced at Lily. "Hear that?"

She nodded, swallowing.

"What is it?"

She shook her head, shrugging.

"It sounds like the house is breathing," he said.

She gave another nod, swallowing once more. Then her eyes grew large, and larger . . . her mouth opened wide, and wider . . . and she pointed to something behind him with a brown, shaking finger.

Marco whirled in his seat. On a shelf high against the wall, books were moving. As the boy and girl stared, a book edged slowly out and dropped from the shelf, landing with a thud on the floor. Another fell immediately behind it, followed by a third, a fourth.

Lily gasped. The boy tightened, grasping TNT in both fists.

"*Merr-ow!*"

Curious Cat raised up on the shelf, humping his black back and stretching. He gazed down at the pair with his golden eyes, black tail swishing. Then he leaned over the edge of the shelf, claws gripping the books below. After a pause, as if for effect, he sprang to the top of the desk and from there to the floor, remarking, "*Rrrow!*"

"*Gungah!*"

"Brother!"

Curious Cat walked carefully out of the room, calling over his black shoulder, "*Merr-ow!*"

"Let's follow him," Marco whispered.

"I'm with you." Lily sounded as if she didn't want to be left alone.

Curious Cat went straight to the staircase on that side of the house. At the bottom, he crouched, black tail curling all the way up over his back, then uncurling all the way down to the floor.

"*Merr-ow!*"

He pounced upon the third step, stopped, glanced back with his glowing eyes, like a pair of tiny moons, and added, "*Rrrow!*"

He bounded up to the seventh step and again called a halt, waiting for the boy and girl to set foot on the staircase.

"*Merr-ow!*"

Tail swishing, claws scratching on the bare wood, Curious Cat went all the way to the top this time. Then he turned completely around and watched the girl and boy as they climbed slowly after him, urging them on with a hearty "*Merr-ow!*"

At the top of the stairs, Marco noticed a strange coldness. Curious Cat turned to the left, and walked up to a wooden door that was in serious need of paint—paint of any color. The ceiling and walls around it were stained—and stained again, and again.

Marco followed the leader. Lily was right with him, her fingers clutching his arm. Outside Shady Hall, the wind roared; the rain pounded and hammered.

At the door, Curious Cat rose up on his hind legs, claws scraping on the wood, and stretched, *s-t-r-e-t-c-h-e-d*, glancing up at the boy, at the girl, at the boy.

"*Merr-ow!*"

Marco tried the door. Locked. Locked as if the key had been turned there for the last time a century or more ago. The boy crouched down and peered through the keyhole. In the dim, stormy afternoon light he could see nothing but an old, black, iron fireplace.

Cold air was coming from the keyhole into his face, bringing with it a series of soft noises—a fluttering, a squeaking, as if mice had set up a village inside. He also noticed a damp, musty smell that nearly made him sneeze.

"*Merr-ow!*"

Behind him a board groaned.

"This was my great-grandmother's room, Marco," Hazel Danton told him. "It hasn't been used since she died during the War Between the States."

9

THE CURSE OF THE DANTONS

Lily gave a startled cry at the sudden appearance of her great-aunt. If Marco hadn't been a boy without fear, he would have gasped, or shuddered—at or least shivered. It was not the most pleasant thing in the world to be in a tense situation, and have someone suddenly and quietly come up behind you.

He rubbed his head, smoothing down the hairs that had prickled on the back of his neck.

"I'm sorry," Miss Danton said. "I didn't mean to scare you."

"You didn't scare me," the boy replied.

"Huh!" Lily added. "Me, n-neither."

"Miss Hazel," Marco asked, "do you have a key to this room?"

"Must be one around here somewhere," she replied. "We've had no reason to use the room—I believe I told you the fireplace has never worked since the Yankee shell hit the chimney. We've generally avoided this part of the house."

Cold, water-stained, musty, it seemed a good place to avoid. Following Curious Cat, the three walked up the hall, away from the grim, paintless door. Initials, along with the dates 1864 and 1865, were scratched on the walls.

"The Yankee occupation troops," Miss Danton explained.

"Hey, what's this?" Marco stooped down to examine the wooden floor, where someone—probably with a bayonet—

yeah, it must have been a bayonet—had spent a good deal of time carefully carving out the words "Liberty and Union."

"You'll have to ask Mr. Cooper about that," Miss Hazel replied. "I'm sure he would know. He should be back from Vicksburg this afternoon, if the storm doesn't hold him up."

Outside, rain thudded against the walls, and the rising wind gave the windows a good shaking.

"You haven't seen the rest of the house, have you, Marco?" Miss Danton said. "Come along. I'll take you on the grand tour. Lily wouldn't be interested. She has seen all this."

Lily hugged herself with her round arms, glancing over her shoulder. "Oh, I'd love to see it again," she replied.

Miss Hazel stopped in the hall before a life-size portrait of a stern-looking man in a blue uniform with gold trimming. His right hand on his sword.

"That's Jacques Danton, my great-great-great-grand-father," she said. "He fought with Andrew Jackson at the Battle of New Orleans. He's the one who built Shady Hall. Looks like he's coming right out of the wall, doesn't he?"

"Sure does," Marco agreed.

"He was killed by a panther in Big Green Swamp, just a few years after Shady Hall was completed. "This," she went on, showing the boy a smaller picture over the mantelpiece in one of the bedrooms, "was his daughter Marie. She was lost with her husband when the schooner *General Winters* went down off Trinidad in 1827. Sunk by pirates, the story goes. . . .

"And this was Jacques Danton's son, John, the one who's supposed to have built the family fortune. 'Hard Money Johnny,' he was called. Look at that face!"

A man with narrow eyes under thick eyebrows and a tight mouth, pressed down by a long mustache, glared out of the heavy, gold-painted frame. He had the appearance of someone who had little to say in life, except maybe, "Pay up!"

"He died of Bronze John—yellow fever—in 1856," Miss Hazel continued. "This was his oldest son, Willard, when he was a boy about your age, Marco. Willard didn't live long enough to have an adult portrait painted."

She paused, sighing.

"He's the one my heart has always gone out to, Marco. When he was twenty, he married a girl from Charleston, and had hardly brought her home to Shady Hall when he had to fight a duel."

"With Roy Knee," the boy said.

"Roy Knee," she nodded. "According to the family story I always heard, he made some remark about the Danton money having come from smuggling and highway robbery—that has always been the rumor, you know. But Roy Knee said what he did at a big country dance, in front of a crowd of people, and Willard struck him—smack in the face. Right there, Roy Knee challenged Willard to a duel.

"Dueling was against the law by that time. In this part of the country, though, it was still considered the only way gentlemen could settle a quarrel. The fact that Roy Knee was a crack shot and Willard was a very poor one made no difference in the 'gentlemen's code.' Willard's bride begged him not to go through with the duel, but, of course, he had to, or he would have been branded a coward for the rest of his life.

"Willard and his seconds were to meet the Roy Knee party at seven in the morning, at the Orange Grove, a dreary spot on the other side of Bayou Terrebonne. It was pistols at ten paces.

"'If I escape injury,' Willard told his bride, 'I'll send a messenger on a white horse. If I fall to Roy Knee's fire, the messenger will come on a black horse.'"

"Show Marco the balcony, Aunt Hazel," Lily urged.

Miss Danton opened a door, and took the two young people out on the second-floor veranda, at the back of the house. Shreds of dark clouds were still racing across the gray sky; and wet, unhappy swamp animals continued to troop north along Bayou Terrebonne.

"Willard's bride stood here, waiting," Miss Danton told them. "Waiting," she added. "Waiting. . . . At last, about seven-thirty she heard galloping hoofbeats coming along the far bank of the bayou, and then the messenger appeared. The horse was black!"

"*Gungah!*"

"Then the girl either jumped to those flagstones below, or fainted and fell. Either way, she was killed."

"*Gungah!*"

"Wait, that's not all," Lily told Marco. "Go on, Aunt Hazel."

"Let's get back inside—Willard hadn't been killed outright, but he was badly wounded," Miss Danton went on, closing the door behind them. "They had to probe—you know, search—for the bullet. Willard died three days later, without ever regaining consciousness."

"*Gungah!*"

"Will you *wait!*" his cousin exclaimed. "Go on, Aunt Hazel."

"Willard's eighteen-year-old brother Jeremy, was a much better shot than he. Jeremy took the bullet that the doctor had removed from Willard's body and held it high. 'This ball,' he said, 'will kill Roy Knee!' "

"*Gun—*" Marco began, then caught the look from his cousin.

"Jeremy challenged, Roy Knee accepted. The Orange Grove at seven. Pistols at ten paces. At the first fire, Jeremy put his bullet in the center of Roy Knee's forehead."

"*Gungah!*"

Lily grabbed a handful of her hair and twisted it like a rope around her neck.

"Cousin Marco," she snapped, "will you please stop making that silly noise and *listen?*"

"I thought she was through," the boy replied. "This is *some* exciting."

Miss Hazel continued. "People said Jeremy had murdered him—although nobody seemed to be upset that Roy Knee had murdered Willard. Anyway, next morning, when Jeremy came downstairs, he found a black candle burning outside the front door of Shady Hall."

"A black candle?" Marco repeated.

"Voodoo," Lily told him.

"Voodoo!" the boy glanced at his cousin.

"Yes, *voodoo*," Lily said. "Aunt Hazel is finished, Marco," she added. "Now you can say '*Gungah*' all you want to."

The boy turned back to Hazel Danton.

"Someone, probably Roy Knee's father, Earl Knee, got a voodoo doctor to lay a curse on Shady Hall," she told him.

Marco shook his head.

"But, Miss Hazel, you don't believe in voodoo—do you?"

"No, although right many people around here used to. When Jeremy's horse threw him not long afterward, and Jeremy died of a broken neck, people said it was the curse working. But I kind of suspect Earl Knee was close by with a slingshot when that horse reared."

"*Gungah!*"

"Aunt Hazel," Lily exclaimed, "you never told me that!"

"Here's Jim," her great-aunt said. "Isn't he good-looking?"

They had come to Hazel Danton's bedroom. She picked up a framed snapshot from the nightstand by the four-poster bed and handed it to Marco.

It showed Jim Danton at the tiller of his sailboat, smiling up at the camera. He was not bad looking, but also not good looking. He was nice looking, the boy decided. In other words, he looked like a nice guy. Jim Danton was almost completely bald, with a big round nose and a wide mouth. His large eyes were set wide apart and deep in his head. They were the best thing about him.

Hazel Danton carefully put the snapshot back on the nightstand. As they all returned to the hallway, she remarked, almost to herself, "It's so sad he had to die that way."

The boy kept remembering those two duels. Something about them was wrong, but he couldn't think what. He stood with Miss Hazel, her grandniece and Curious Cat under the painted eyes of deceased Dantons. The sense of the long history of violent deaths felt like eleven pounds pressing on his shoulders.

With a loud, insistant splatter, bands of rain streamed down the bedroom windows, throwing their squirming shadows on the nearby wall. There was a long, low sigh. Marco glanced up at Miss Danton. But she wasn't sighing, she was listening. So was her grandniece.

Slowly the sound died away . . . and there was only the noisy splatter of the rain on the windows.

"Miss Hazel," the boy said, "last night you told me that it's easier to hear the past than it is to see it."

She gazed down at him. "Yes?"

"That breathing sound just now—you must have heard it before—do you think it's from the past?"

"I don't know, Marco. Could be. Might very well be. It's just as I told you last night—a house like Shady Hall, where so many people of the same family have lived and died, is bound to have some traces of them. An inheritance of living and thinking that is passed on from one generation to another, almost as if it were breathed in the very air. Do you understand what I mean?"

"I don't know, ma'am." The boy rubbed his head. "Miss Hazel, do you think many other people around here know the way you feel?"

"I used to discuss it with my brother Jim," she replied. "I expect I mentioned it to Antoine Boudier a time or two. And Dr. Labuisse and I used to talk about it."

"Miss Hazel, who's Dr. Labuisse?"

"The family doctor."

"I thought Dr. Slade was," the boy said.

"He is now. He came out from New Orleans, and took over about three years ago, when Dr. Labuisse went to Arizona for his health. Anyway, I've never made a secret of how I felt. Also, things have a way of getting around in a town like New Paris—especially anything to do with the Dantons and Shady Hall."

"They sure do," Marco agreed.

"Miss Hazel," the boy asked, "when did this funny business start at Shady Hall?"

"Well, I've heard strange noises as far back as I can remember," she replied. "But they didn't really start getting to me until about a year ago."

"After your brother died?" Marco asked.

She nodded.

"When did you start getting the letters?"

"About the same time."

"Ma'am, who do you think they're from?"

Hazel Danton's eyes seemed extra-dark and sunken in her white face.

"I don't know, I don't know. I just wish they'd stop!"

"*Merr-ow!*"

For sometime, Curious Cat had been sitting like a black

statue, but now he stood up, stretched, and walked stiff-legged up the hall to a door, tail swishing.

"That leads to the attic, Marco," Hazel Danton told the boy. "There's nothing to see up there."

"*Merr-ow!*" The black cat sat at the door, gazing up at the three human beings with eyes like a pair of gold nuggets in his black face. "*Rrrow!*"

"Oh, all right, Curious Cat," Miss Danton said, opening the door. "If you insist."

The animal scampered up the dark, narrow staircase, and the three humans followed, with the old wooden stairs crying out at each footstep. Rain landing on the shingles overhead sounded like thousands of drumming fingers, playing from one end of the roof to the other, then back again.

Pale, watery light came through the gabled windows. The attic was filled with odds and ends from a hundred and fifty years—dolls, teddy bears, a rocking chair, a rocking horse, lamp shades, a sewing machine, a fly swatter, and trunks like treasure chests that, Miss Hazel showed Lily and Marco, were filled with neatly folded clothes.

"*Merr-ow!*"

Curious Cat trotted over to a stack of large canvases leaning against the rough timbers of one wall. Slowly, Marco went through the stack. It was a collection of paintings—and very good ones, too, he thought—of streets, rivers, beaches, people.

"Jim brought those home with him from France," Miss Danton told him. "Painting was his life until he returned to Shady Hall."

Marco noticed something written on the back of a canvas. The figure $1,000 was crossed out and $750 was put under it. But that was also crossed out and $500 was written below. Then that was crossed out, and there were no more figures.

"Jim had his pride," Hazel Danton commented. "These

paintings—every one of them—took him months to do. But he couldn't sell a single one for a halfway decent price, and he refused to go any lower. Folks will pay top dollar for the strangest things, like stamps and dishes, but they're just not interested in paintings by an unknown artist."

"I think these are great," Marco told her.

She smiled. "I do, too."

"So do I," Lily agreed emphatically.

"I've wanted so badly to have them framed so they could be hung downstairs," Miss Hazel remarked sadly. "But I just haven't had the money."

"Merr-ow!"

Curious Cat was sitting by an easel at the north window, as if posing for his portrait. On the stand was a painting of a big, dark house.

"Why, that's Shady Hall!" Miss Hazel exclaimed. "Jim must have done it after he came home!"

The three studied the work. It was difficult to see in the dim light, but Marco noticed that the entire painting was done in thousands and thousands of different-colored dots. There was something about that picture. . . . It had a spooky nature, and gave the feeling that it was more than just the painting of a house.

"Funny, Jim didn't mention that to me," Miss Danton remarked as they started back to the stairs.

"Sheriff Gross said your brother was secretive," the boy told her.

Miss Hazel's eyes flashed.

"Sammy Gross," she snapped. "What does *he* know? Anyway, he's dead wrong. Jim minded his own business, and expected other folks to mind theirs—not that they did, of course. Jim had his own way of doing things, and the good people of New Paris didn't approve—like when Jim had his funeral at dawn."

That picture of Shady Hall had a spooky nature, and gave the feeling that it was more than just the painting of a house.

"Yes, Dr. Slade said—"

The boy stopped, realizing his blunder. Miss Danton snatched a fly swatter off the sewing machine, and swished it like a saber.

"We're back to Dr. Slade again!" she exclaimed angrily. "Just you wait until I see that little gossip! Always nosing around, asking personal questions—'How do you feel today?' 'Are you drinking your prune juice?' *Awgh!*"

The fly swatter cut the air once more.

"When he drew up his will about seven years ago," Miss Danton went on, "Jim told me his reason for the dawn burial. 'Only my friends will come to my funeral, and that's all I want,' he said. He was wrong, of course—everyone in New Paris came."

"Except Henri Cassatt," Marco reminded her.

"Except Henri Cassatt," she agreed. "Even Tad Payne was there."

"Miss Hazel," the boy said, "Tad Payne said he put a new battery in your brother's car, 'new plugs, new everything,' and your brother wouldn't pay him."

"He did, did he? He *did*, did he? Let me tell you about that little job. Tad Payne handed Jim a big bill, but Jim found out that he had put in an *old* battery—"

The fly swatter smacked the sewing machine so hard it sounded like a pistol shot.

"*Old* plugs (smack!), old (smack!) *everything!*"

Outside, the wind screamed as if that was what Miss Hazel had been beating, and rain thudded against the side of the house like a huge fist.

"Miss Hazel," Marco asked, as the three humans and Curious Cat started down the attic stairs, "when did your brother begin taking those trips to New York and Washington?"

"Let's see. About seven years ago, I reckon."

"About the same time he made his will?"

"I expect it was."

"Why did you want to know that, Marco?" Lily asked.

"I'm not sure exactly," the boy replied. "I'll have to work on it. Miss Hazel, I know your brother went to Washington to see the people at the National Trust. But do you have any idea why he took all those trips to New York?"

" 'Business' is all he said," Miss Danton answered, shutting the attic door behind them. "I figured it was *his* business and didn't ask further."

"I don't mean to be nosy," Marco told her.

"Huh!" Lily snorted, tossing her hair.

"Of course you don't, Marco. I know that. And we really appreciate your wanting to help clear up this mess, don't we Lily?"

Her grandniece grabbed that hair again, and pushed it over her face. "Sure do."

Curious Cat yawned. All this talk seemed to be boring him. He trotted off, leaving Miss Hazel, her grandniece, and the boy in the corridor, under the eyes of the portraits. A long, low sigh sounded through the house.

It was, Marco thought, as though all these old Dantons were living in the dark, narrow spaces between the walls, staring out at them from the windows of the picture frames.

"I expect Sammy Gross isn't far off when he says Jim was 'secretive,' " Miss Hazel remarked, almost to herself. "Like most artists, Jim lived in his own world, and he didn't want people asking questions—but a finer, kinder man has never set foot on this earth. Jim Danton was a gentle man, and a gentleman."

"I wonder, do you think he went to New York because he could sell his paintings there?" the boy asked.

The Mistress of Shady Hall shook her head sadly.

"All the ones he brought back from France are still up in

the attic," she replied. "He never took anything on those trips but a little old suitcase."

Lily grabbed her cousin by the arm. "Why did you ask about the paintings?"

"I'm trying to figure out where Jim Danton got the money to—how do you say it—*endow* Shady Hall for the National Trust, and also—" He stopped, eyes looking down at the floor.

"Also what?" Lily demanded. "Don't hold out on us, Detective Fennerty, or I'll take your badge away!"

"Also," Miss Hazel supplied the answer, "where Jim thought he was going to get the money for me to live in Florida—isn't that right, Marco?"

"Yes, ma'am."

"I wish I knew," she replied in a soft voice. "I'm sure Jim would have told me sooner or later—if he hadn't been killed. He was like that. Jim was not the type to tell you what he was *going* to do. He'd do it, and *then* he'd tell you."

She gazed off into space, then straightened. Her voice was brisk when she said, "Lily, I expect we'd best cook up a few meals so we won't starve if Hurricane Inez knocks out our gas. Then we've got to fill the tub, and all the pots with fresh water, and collect lanterns and candles."

Like a tall, thin, wobbling tower, she started down the stairs, saying, "Come on, girl, we have work to do!"

"And you, Cousin Marco," Lily called over her shoulder, "go into the study and think about things till we call you for supper."

Marco clicked his heels, saluting.

The study was dark, and he switched on a lamp by Miss Hazel's desk.

"*Merr-ow!*"

Curious Cat lay in Miss Hazel's chair, squinting at the

light. Then he put his paws over his eyes, as if playing hide-and-seek. *"Rrrow!"*

Marco walked around the room, listening to the commotion of the storm, and working on the case. There were so many things to consider, he didn't know where to start—like where did Jim Danton get the money to endow Shady Hall, and where did he plan to get the money to leave his sister? And who is the guy that's writing the letters, and how come they're mailed from all over the United States? And. . . .

The grumpy grandfather clock in the hall struck six. Before it had seemed to be telling him to slow down. Now the message of its chimes was more like, "Get moving!" Nearly half his visiting and sleuthing time gone, Marco thought, and he hadn't *begun* to solve the case.

"Merr-ow!"

Curious Cat jumped down from the chair, and walked slowly out of the study, past the staircase, across the hall to a heavy wooden door. He humped his back, rubbing against the rough wood, and gazed up at the boy with his golden eyes —dead serious, as always.

"Where's that go, Curious Cat?" Marco asked.

"Rrrow!"

"Meaning, 'Open the door and find out'—right?"

The door was bolted by a thick iron bar. The boy drew back the bolt and pulled the door open. The smell of age and dampness and mold, as if from an old grave, came up from the huge black hole. He patted around the cold brick walls inside for a light switch, but found none.

"Wait, let me get my flashlight."

"Rrrow!"

Marco let go of the bolt, and the door slowly shut itself. He ran upstairs to his room, and took the flashlight from his suitcase. When he came back down the stairs, Curious Cat was sitting patiently by the door. The boy pulled it open again, and flashed his light into the hole.

"*Gungah!*"

Dusty cobwebs, spun by ancient, long-dead spiders, hung like torn thin curtains from the brick walls and arched ceiling. There were so many webs—dead moth caught here, dead moth there—that the light could not pierce through. A staircase made of wooden planks, with no railing, led downward to . . . what?

Marco Fennerty, Junior, a boy of eleven years who was without fear, squared his shoulders, tightened his stomach muscles, and took the first step. The webs swayed toward him, and he waved the flashlight in a circle to cut through them.

"Come on, Curious Cat!"

The boy took the second step, the third. Black shadows closed in behind him. The walls were green with mold, and he could hear a swishing as if from water.

"Curious Cat?"

"*Merr-ow!*"

Marco turned. The animal crouched outside the doorway leading to the staircase, watching him with interest. Then he sprang lightly back as the big door swung . . . swung . . . swung —shut.

"*Gungah!*"

But let others retreat. Fearless Fennerty would go forward. Four, five, six, seven, eight, nine—he was at the bottom of the staircase, standing on a brick floor (a rather damp and very moldy brick floor). Cobwebs stretched from the ceiling to a wooden keg by the stairs. On the keg, facing him, was a rat (a rat)!

But it was so dried and shriveled, Marco noticed, that it must have died in 1837 or '39, at least.

Dead ahead was a moldy, damp brick wall. That must be

—it had to be—the entrance of the tunnel leading to Bayou Terror that Miss Hazel's great-grandfather had sealed up during the Civil War. Leaning against it was a long pole, with a hook on the end, such as one of the Danton ancestors might have used to pull a smuggler's rowboat to the bank of Bayou Terror—Bayou *Terrebonne*. Down here, the swishing noise was louder. When Marco put his ear against the cold, damp bricks, the sound was louder yet.

Well, nothing else to see down here. The boy climbed the stairs somewhat faster than he had come down, and gave the door an uncertain push. It opened easily!

"*Merr-ow!*" Curious Cat seemed glad to see him.

"You!" Marco snapped. "Fine friend *you* are!"

The door closed behind him. The boy stalked back into the study, with the animal trotting along beside him, brushing against his leg and going "*Merr-ow!*" and sometimes "*Rrrow!*"

Wind howled in the chimney, and rain dashed against the windows. Marco walked up and down the room, swinging the flashlight, and figuring about things. From the kitchen came the happy sounds of two women at work, along with the smell of food cooking. The boy took a deep breath, glad to get rid of the unpleasant odor from below.

He glanced down at the flashlight, thinking, thinking. Wait a minute. . . . Aha!

It was a long, lonely climb to the attic, but—after that business below—it would be like nothing, Marco told himself. He hurried out of the study to the main staircase. Curious Cat, rolled up in a comfortable black ball on Miss Hazel's chair, made no move to follow.

Nuts to him!

Marco mounted the stairs to the second floor, then walked down the corridor, picking up speed as he passed the watchful eyes of the Dantons, who peered out at him from their "windows." A sigh came. It could have been from the house—then again, it could have come from a boy who went under the name of Marco Fennerty, Junior.

He opened the door to the attic and climbed the complaining steps. The wet, streaming windows sparkled in the light of his flash. Rain, like regiments of rats, (big, live rats) charged across the roof—retreated—charged again.

Shoulders back, stomach in, flashlight in left hand, TNT in right, Marco Fennerty, Junior, marched past the clutter of, he didn't know-how-many generations of the Danton Family, to the easel standing at the north window.

He stood by the rattling window and studied the painting in the light of the flash. Shady Hall, with all its gloomy history, stood out clearly from the tiny dots of paint. But that wasn't all. . . .

As the boy crouched, peering at the house, he saw the features of a man—the center column became a nose, gable windows grew into deep-set eyes.

He was staring into the face of Jim Danton!

10

HURRICANE INEZ

Marco sat in the study, mulling over the personality of Jim Danton and the painting in the attic. He remembered Miss Hazel's remark last night: "How that man loved this house!" This painting, Marco thought, clearly showed how important Shady Hall was to her brother. . . .

"Chow time!" Lily yelled, banging on a pot. "Come and get it!"

The boy arose and went into the dining room. Miss Hazel and her grandniece were already seated, a big platter filled with a pot roast and vegetables in the center of the table.

Lily glanced up at him and screamed, "Marco!"

"Marco!" her great-aunt exclaimed. "What on earth have you been doing?"

"You go wash those hands," Lily commanded. "*And* that face. *And* those ears. And get those stupid old moths out of your hair!"

In the bathroom mirror, Marco saw that he was covered with cobwebs and stuff. He quickly washed up, cleaned the sink, then had another go at the dining room.

"That's better," Lily told him. "You may sit down now."

The boy gave her a deep bow. "Thank you, Miss Lily, ma'am."

"Huh!"

"From the looks of you before, I expect you were exploring the cellar," Miss Hazel remarked. "Find anything of interest?"

"No, ma'am," he replied. Then he told them about the face in the painting.

"We'll have to go have us a look," Miss Danton said. "Not tonight, though. Too much to do."

Wind seemed to nudge Shady Hall with a monstrous shoulder, and rain crashed like a sea against the outer walls. The lights in the chandelier flickered, went out, flickered again, then blacked out completely. The trio ate by the soft glow of a hurricane lamp. If anything, it made the meal taste better.

Outside, the tires of an automobile crunched on the shell driveway, and headlights flashed through the dining room windows as the car drove around to the back of the house.

"Mr. Cooper," Miss Danton told the others, "back from Vicksburg."

"Now then," Lily instructed her cousin when they had finished eating, "you go into the study and work on things while Aunt Hazel and I do the dishes. And Marco," she added firmly, "we expect you to come up with something."

The boy walked around and around the study, thinking so hard his head hurt. He rubbed it gently, hoping that would make the thoughts flow. He remembered the fairy tale *Rumpelstiltskin*, and the miller's daughter, who was put into a room filled with straw and ordered to spin it into gold. The trouble was, he had no little dwarf to help him come up with something.

"*Merr-ow!*"

Curious Cat ambled into the room, quite well satisfied from the supper of chicken livers that Miss Hazel had told Marco was provided for in her brother's will. The animal walked slowly over to the desk, jumped upon it and, from there, leaped up to a bookshelf. He lay on his side, head raised to see the boy, then closed his eyes and sank back with a "*Rrrow!*"

Marco went to the desk, opened it, and began to go over the letters. One was postmarked "Pittsburgh, Pennsylvania," a second "Cairo, Illinois," a third "Natchez, Mississippi."

Mississippi, the boy thought. Wait a minute—wait a minute! He searched the shelves until he found an Atlas, then turned it to a map of the United States. *Gungah!*

"Marco," he exclaimed softly, raising both hands high, "Marco Fennerty, Junior!"

Curious Cat raised up, asking "*Rrrow?*"

The boy studied the grim messages inside the envelopes, paying particular attention to the handwriting.

Get out of that house

That house is cursed

Hmmm. That would mean, that had to mean, it had no choice but mean . . .

"Okay, Marco, what's the deal?" Lily demanded from the doorway.

"Oh, come in, dear cousin," the boy invited her with another bow. "I believe, I have come up with one or two small items that might interest you."

"Like?"

"All the letters were written by the same guy."

"Impossible!"

He spread out the letters on the floor, and they both crouched down.

"Look at the 'g' in 'get' and the 'h' in 'house,' " he told her. "See the way the 'o' and the 'a' have those little loops? Look at how he makes the 'f' in 'of'. I'm telling you, the same guy is writing all the letters."

"Okay, but how does he jump all around the country, and still have time to be in New Paris so much, if you're so smart?"

"He has a buddy who works on a Mississippi River towboat," Marco replied.

His cousin grabbed a thick strand of her hair, and tossed it over one shoulder, sitting back on her heels.

"Marco Fennerty!" she exclaimed. "How could you *possibly* know *that?*"

"Because all these letters were mailed from river towns on the Mississippi," he explained. "Look at the map. I figure the guy we're looking for writes a mess of letters, then gives them to his buddy to mail, one at a time, and his towboat stops along the way to pick up or drop off barges on the Mississippi— or the Missouri and the Ohio. Both," he added, "being in the Mississippi River system."

Lily gave him a suspicious look. Then she crouched, even lower, studying the map, checking and rechecking the postmarks on the envelopes. At last she straightened up, and pulled her hair back from her face with both hands, revealing a grin.

"Cousin Marco, you are brilliant," she said slowly and softly. "Hey, Aunt Hazel!" she yelled. "Come in and shake hands with my brilliant cousin!"

The boy stood up, looking down to hide his pleased smile, as Lily explained his discoveries to her great-aunt.

"There's still a mess of stuff I have to find out," he told them. "Miss Danton, is it okay if I go over to see Mr. Cooper?"

"In this weather?" she asked. "Can't you wait till to-morrow?"

"We're running out of time," he told her.

"I'm going, too," Lily said.

"No, you're not, Miss Priss," her great-aunt replied. "Wait, Marco, let me get Jim's foul weather gear for you."

"Wish I was a boy," Lily said.

Marco felt like a knight being dressed for battle, as Miss Danton and his sulky cousin helped him on with the oilskin coat. Miss Hazel lowered the sou'wester onto his head with both hands, as if it were a helmet. He pulled the rubber boots on himself.

"Don't stay, Marco," Miss Danton urged. "We need a man in the house tonight."

The boy stepped out of the study door into the roaring, pouring night. An almost solid mass of gray was rushing across the sky from east to west. The beam of the flashlight showed that the dancing water of Bayou Terrebonne was overflowing its banks. Feet slipping in the big boots, the boots themselves sliding on the drenched grass, one hand gripping the sou'-wester, the other his flash, Marco pushed his way across the yard to the cottage and knocked at the door.

"Marco!" Eugene Gerard exclaimed when he had opened the door and recognized who was standing there, in spite of the storm and the sou'wester. He had a lighted candle in one hand, and a dishtowel in the other.

"It's me," the younger boy agreed, while rain poured from his head covering as if from the spout of a pitcher. "I'd like to ask your father a few questions," he explained as the other boy helped him out of the dripping oilskins.

"Ask him *anything*," Eugene Gerard said. "He knows *everything*."

A small man in lounging robe and slippers came in from

another room, the candlelight flashing on his glasses.

"Dad, this is my friend, Marco Fennerty, Junior, from New Orleans," his son said. "Marco, this is my father."

Eugene Gerard introduced his father in the same proud way, Marco thought, as he, himself, introduced Sergeant Fennerty. While he and Mr. Cooper shook hands Eugene Gerard returned to the kitchen.

"Come into the den, Marco," the man said, waving him to a room something like the study at Shady Hall, only smaller.

A desk lighted by a lantern, and covered with papers was in one corner, along with a typewriter on a metal stand. Tolliver was lying in front of the fire, panting. He wagged his tail at Marco once, then whined.

"Easy, fella," Mr. Cooper soothed, petting him. "Tolliver doesn't appreciate this weather one bit," he explained. "I must admit, I kind of like it myself."

"Me, too," Marco replied, and Eugene Gerard yelled agreement, from the kitchen, over the clatter of dishes.

Marco and Mr. Cooper sat across the desk from each other. Mr. Cooper took off his glasses and snapped them shut. "Now then, Detective Marco Fennerty, what can Cal Cooper of the U.S. Army Corps of Engineers do for you?"

"I'd like a little information."

"Ask him *anything*!" Eugene Gerard called, and his father grinned.

"First," Marco told Mr. Cooper, "Miss Hazel Danton said you could tell me what those words carved in the floor upstairs at Shady Hall are all about."

"'Liberty and Union?' They're from a speech Daniel Webster, the Senator from Massachusetts, made during his famous debate with Senator Robert Young Hayne of South Carolina over states' rights in 1830. His speech ended, 'Liberty and Union, now and forever, one and inseparable!'"

"What'd I tell you, Marco?" Eugene Gerard shouted with pride.

"Thank you, sir," the boy said. "Mr. Cooper, you know the story about the duel that Willard Danton fought with Roy Knee?"

"Miss Danton told me."

"Well, I read a book about dueling once, and it seems to me, that the guy who's challenged can pick the weapon he wants to fight with," Marco went on.

"Right. According to the original Code Duello, as practiced by the French and Spanish, the people who first lived in Louisiana, the challenged party has the choice of weapons— pistols. fencing swords, sabers."

"Then, if Willard Danton was such a bad shot and Roy Knee was such a good one, why didn't Mr. Danton pick a weapon like, swords so he'd have a fighting chance?"

"You see, Marco, the Americans who came into this area toward the end of the eighteenth century changed the Code Duello to suit themselves, since fighting with swords is not part of the American tradition. Gentlemen inevitably met on the Field of Honor armed with pistols."

"So Willard Danton had no choice," the boy said softly.

Mr. Cooper opened his spectacles, and shut them with a snap. "He could have picked shotguns."

"*Shotguns? Gungah!*"

"He probably figured he had a better chance of survival if hit by a pistol ball," Mr. Cooper went on. "One of the good things about the Civil War was, that it made people realize how stupid it was to settle an argument by standing thirty feet apart and banging away at each other. Killing is killing, no matter how politely you go about it. The battlefields at Antietam, Gettysburg, and all made the Field of Honor look a little silly."

"How about *that* now, man?" Eugene Gerard called. "Ask him another!"

"I'm almost through," Marco called back. "Mr. Cooper, you've heard the story that there's a mess of money supposed to be hidden at Shady Hall."

"I have."

"Well, if it's true, why would anyone take the chance of keeping all his money in his house—when he might get robbed, or the house burn down, or something? Wouldn't it be smarter and safer to keep it in the bank?"

Again, Mr. Cooper slowly opened his spectacles . . . then snapped them shut.

"It would today," he replied. "But we're talking about a time when the United States was young and growing, and things were more uncertain."

"I'm not sure I understand, sir."

"It's rather complicated, but I'll try to make it as simple as possible. Shady Hall was built shortly before the War of 1812. After the war, the Americans started to push westward, with people borrowing all kinds of money from banks, and each other to pay for land, wagons, horses, supplies, and so on —passing around notes like a blizzard of I.O.U.'s, with nothing much to back them. All right so far?"

"Yes, sir."

"Then came the Panic of 1819, when everyone suddenly became worried about the actual value of these notes, and about the whole financial structure of the United States. Many started to make runs on the banks, to change the notes and their paper money into specie. The banks didn't have enough specie to payoff all this stuff; and all over the country banks failed, and people went broke. The Panic of 1837 was even worse."

"Mr. Cooper," Marco asked, "what's 'specie'?"

"Coins."

"*Coins?*" the boy repeated in surprise. "You mean like pennies, and nickels, and quarters—things like that?"

"No, Marco, we're talking about coins of gold and silver, as they used to be made in the old days," Mr. Cooper explained. "Coins that were worth one, fifty, a hundred dollars—whatever was stamped on them—because of the value of the gold and silver that was in them—the so-called 'hard' money. During the Panics, everything else was considered just so much paper, no matter what amount of dollars was printed on it. People went after that 'hard' money."

The boy swallowed, his voice tight: " 'Hard' money like in 'Hard Money Johnny'?"

"Like in Hard Money Johnny," Mr. Cooper agreed.

"*Hmm*, I'll have to work on this," the boy said. "Thanks very much, sir. You've been a big help."

"What'd I tell you, man, what'd I tell you?" Eugene Gerard yelled from the kitchen.

The storm hadn't grown any worse, but it hadn't grown any better. Rain by the bucketful dashed against the windows, and the wind hissed like a gang of cobras around the eaves.

"American history is great, isn't it?" Mr. Cooper remarked as he walked to the door with the boy. "I've been interested in it since grammar school, but I didn't actually start writing on historical subjects, until eight years ago, when Eugene Gerard's mother died, and I didn't know what to do with myself. I think these old plantation houses are absolutely fascinating. I hope the reading public agrees when my book comes out."

"I hope so, too," Marco agreed. "Good night, Mr. Cooper, and thanks again." He raised his voice. "See you, Eugene Gerard!"

"See you, Marco!"

Marco stepped out of the door, and promptly was struck in the face by a large quantity of rain water. Leaning forward,

The yellow beam of Marco's flashlight shone on the tragic history of the Danton family.

he started to slog toward the big house, whose tiny lights glowed fuzzily through the rain. Then, he thought of something and turned, rocking like a galleon in the wind.

The tragic history of the Dantons was neatly laid out in the headstones of the family cemetery. The yellow beam of the boy's flashlight, shot through and through with golden streaks of rain, shone on the grave of Jacques Danton. Next to it, was the grave of his widow. Then, came the headstone of someone named Sophie Danton, and then a stone whose inscription was clogged with mud and leaves.

Marco crouched down and drew his finger through the letters and numbers.

JEAN DANTON
1798-1856

Next to that was the grave of Willard Danton, which was followed by that of his brother, Jeremy. Who was this woman named Jean Danton, the boy wondered, and where was Hard Money Johnny buried?

11

A FACE AT THE WINDOW

"Marco Fennerty," his cousin called from the study door, "you come in here this instant and stop playing around in that graveyard!"

"I'd like to point out that I wasn't 'playing around in that graveyard,'" the boy told her rather sharply, when he was inside the house and had taken off his dripping foul-weather gear. "I was looking for a clue."

"Wish I was a boy," Lily said, almost to herself. "They have all the fun."

"Did you find a clue, Marco?" Miss Danton asked.

"I'm not sure," he replied. "I was looking for John Danton's grave, but it's not out there."

"He's there, next to his wife Sophie, who died in childbirth. The child, a daughter, was born dead. She's buried with her mother. According to the family history, the father thought a separate headstone for the child was a needless expense, since she didn't even have a name. He never got over that double blow, and was a bitter man the rest of his life."

"Then, Jean Danton is Hard Money Johnny?" the boy asked.

"Yes, only it's not 'Jean' like the girl's name," she told him. "The French for 'John' is spelled J-E-A-N and is pronounced *Zyohn.*"

"Ah!" Marco nodded.

"My people were French, but decided they were Americans after the Battle of New Orleans," Miss Hazel went on.
"Willard and Jeremy both changed their names from whatever the French had been, but Jean kept his, although he was
always known as John."

"Cousin Marco," Lily demanded, "is *that* all you found
out?"

"No, Cousin Lily, not quite," the boy snapped. He passed
on all he had learned from Mr. Cooper.

"So," Marco said, "John Danton lived through the Panic
of 1819 and 1837. He probably thought banks were bad places
to keep money in, and that the only money worth holding
onto in the first place was the coin kind."

"So that's how he got his nickname," Miss Danton said.
"Funny I never thought of that."

"So if there *is* any money hidden in Shady Hall," the boy
added, "it's in gold and silver coins."

His cousin's face had an expression, as if she were about
to sit down to a seven-course dinner. Rubbing her hands together, she urged, "Let's start looking!"

"Tomorrow," Miss Hazel told her. "But, really, children,
I don't expect we'll find anything."

The hurricane was steadily increasing in violence. Wind
shoved against the house, shoved, and shoved again, like a
bully trying to pick a fight. The branches of the oaks banged
together, and sometimes broke off with the report of cannon
shots. The crashing of the bamboo sounded like volleys of
musket fire. Then, from somewhere below, there came a
muffled noise like buried thunder.

The three went from room to room on the first floor,
making sure no doors had been blown open, no windows
broken. Peering through the rain-blurred pane of the living-
room window, Marco saw that some wires were down in the

road, twisting about like snakes, flaring, spitting out great blue and orange sparks.

The grandfather clock in the hall, for all its grumpy nature, seemed to be enjoying the storm. As the trio passed it on the way back to the study, Marco noticed that the hands pointed to ten minutes aften ten. The clock reminded him of one of the smiling faces Lily had drawn in the letter he had received—when was it? Just yesterday!

"*Merr-ow!*"

Curious Cat, like Tolliver, was not enjoying the storm at all. He lay curled up—in as tiny a black ball as he could make—on the bookshelf, his long, black tail twiching nervously everytime the wind launched a fresh assault upon the house. His eyes, in the light of the hurricane lamp, glowed like a pair of little moons.

Marco stooped down, and picked up the books that the animal, in stretching, had knocked off the shelf earlier, checking their titles as he replaced them: *The Spirit World, Life Beyond the Grave, Rare Coins of the Old World and the New.* One book, an aged one with a leather cover, had no title. It seemed to be a diary—something he'd have to check tomorrow, when the light was better, the boy decided.

"Marco," Lily said, "you don't think Curious Cat is the one that knocked all the books off the shelves that time Aunt Hazel and I were at the movie"—she took a deep breath—"do you?"

She was watching him closely. So was her great-aunt.

"I don't believe so," the boy replied. "I believe it was whoever it is that's writing the letters, and pulling all the other funny business here."

"Who?" the wind seemed to be asking. "*Who-o-o-o?*"

The howled question grew louder, even louder and more demanding as the hurricane drew nearer to Shady Hall. Lily

nd her great-aunt sat facing each other silently, except to say
rom time to time, "Listen to that wind!" Curious Cat kept
nuttering, *"Merr-ow!"* and *"Rrrow!"*

Marco paced up and down the study, working on possible
clues without coming up with anything. The grandfather
clock struck eleven, letting the three know it was time they
were all in bed. But they continued to stay up . . . and the
storm wouldn't go away.

Ever so often, the breathing noise sounded through the
house. Nobody commented upon it, but that weird sound
seemed to bother Lily and her great-aunt (although not Curious Cat) more than the storm. Marco was glancing through the
coin book when the strange rumble sounded again from below.

"What *is* that?" Miss Hazel asked.

"Yeah!" Lily agreed, sitting up straight.

"Rrrow!"

Marco's cousin and her great-aunt were both staring at
him, and he could feel Curious Cat's eyes on the back of his
head.

"I'm sorry, I don't know," the boy admitted.

Lily groaned, slumping back in her chair. He had let her
down.

Face afire with embarrassment and irritation, Marco
studied *Rare Coins of the Old World and the New.* . . . Wait a
minute, wait a minute—*Gungah!*

"Hey, y'all, listen to this!" he exclaimed.

Holding the book close to the hurricane lamp, he read
aloud, " 'Students of early American coins often make the mis-
take of concentrating on New England and the Eastern Sea-
board. They should take a good look at Louisiana and its
Queen City, New Orleans. New Orleans was founded in 1718
by . . . blah, blah, blah; blah, blah, blah—"

"Marco," Lily interrupted, "we can do without all the

blah, blah, blahs."

"Listen," he told her, and continued reading, " 'The dis
covery of gold and silver in the West and the difficulty of trans
porting large quantities of bullion—' Miss Hazel, what'
'bullion'?"

"Bars of gold and silver."

" 'The difficulty of transporting large quantities of (gold
and silver bars) through country menaced by bandits and
hostile Indians resulted in the founding of a number of local
mints. The New Orleans mint was founded in 1836, and began
to produce coins two years later.

" 'All coins produced in New Orleans bear the mint mark
"O." The New Orleans mint turned out both gold and silver
coins from 1838 to 1909. It was seized by the Confederate gov
ernment at the start of the Civil War—' "

"Cousin Marco," Lily broke in, "we wish to thank you
for this fascinating lesson in American history."

"Just *listen*," he insisted, turning the page. "*Gungah!* 'One
of the rarest of all United States coins is the so-called "Smil
ing Liberty," which was produced in New Orleans from 1838
to 1840. This gold coin bears the head of a woman with a
definite smile on her face, and the date—always between those
years. The reverse bears a spread eagle and the stamp: "Fifty
dolls." '

"That must mean 'fifty dollars,' " Marco said.

"So what?" Lily demanded.

"So I think Hard Money Johnny kept all the 'Smiling
Liberty' coins, along with all the other gold and silver coins
he could latch on to."

"But, Marco," Lily pointed out, "it would take a heap of
even fifty-dollar coins to make very much money."

"The thing is," he told her, "these coins are worth much
more than fifty dollars apiece to collectors. It says in this book

that one would be worth anywhere from five thousand to twenty-five thousand dollars, depending on how much wear it had. 'A "Smiling Liberty" in "very fine" or "mint" condition,' " he read aloud, 'could demand a king's ransom.' "

"Brother!" Lily exclaimed.

"Yes," Miss Hazel agreed. "It wouldn't take many of those to add up to a tidy sum. But, Marco, as I recall, the federal government made everyone turn in their gold in the 1930s. To have gold coins today would be against the law."

"Wait, I saw something about that earlier," the boy said. "Ah, here it is: 'Rare and unusual gold coins may be retained in any quantity by collectors, according to the President's Order Number 6260.' "

"What number was that again?" his cousin asked.

"Number sixty-two—oh, come on, Lily!" he exploded, seeing her too-innocent face. "Miss Hazel, somebody has drawn a circle around the page that tells about the 'Smiling Liberty,' and I'm guessing it was your brother."

"Expect you're right. *I* didn't do it."

"I'm also guessing that your brother found out where Hard Money Johnny had hidden all his dough. If that's correct, we know why your brother made all those trips to New York, and where he got the money to endow Shady Hall for the National Trust."

"You mean he went to New York to sell the stuff to coin dealers," Lily said. "Why didn't he do it all at once—too heavy to carry?"

"I expect he did it little by little to keep the price up," her great-aunt told her. "Don't you reckon, Marco?"

"That's the way I figure," he agreed. "Also, if what Mr. Boudier says about what your brother was planning to leave you is true, there's still two hundred thousand dollars worth of coins still hidden in Shady Hall."

Lily tossed her hair back impatiently. "Come on, why wait till tomorrow? Let's start looking now!" she urged.

"Hush, child," Miss Hazel said. "Wait! What was that?"

Hurricane Inez was hurling itself full force upon Shady Hall, but that's not what Miss Hazel meant. For, over the roar of the wind and the drumming of the rain, there came to their ears a soft, secretive sound, a rattle that had nothing to do with the storm.

Miss Danton's face was white. "Somebody's trying to get in the hall window!"

Grabbing his flashlight, Marco ran out into the dark hall. This was one of the windows, whose lock he and Eugene Gerard had replaced. Marco held his thumb on the flash button, ready to snap on the beam. The rattling had stopped, but now it started again—soft, slow, sneaky.

Standing against the wall, the boy inched his head out until his right eye could see through the window pane. In the darkness outside, he could make out a darker shape, crouched at the window. Marco took a deep breath, then knocked on the pane sharply with his fist. At the same time, he snapped on the flashlight.

The beam caught the face of someone in a poncho and rain hat, who was glancing up in surprise at Marco's knock.

That face! It did not belong to a human being. It was deathly white, with black holes for eyes and huge, tusk-like teeth. Marco staggered back as if hit in the chest, his breath hissing out. In the next second or so he was back at the window, but that horrible thing was gone.

"Marco!" Miss Hazel gasped. "Where are you going?"

"Going to get the Coopers and Tolliver," he told her, pulling on his boots. "Why don't you call Sheriff Gross and Dr. Slade?"

He buttoned his oilskin coat and pulled his sou'wester

down on his head. "Lock the door after me."

"Be careful!" Miss Danton gasped.

"Glad I'm *not* a boy," Lily said.

Marco stepped outside. The study door was promptly shut behind him, and the bolt shot home. Of course, he was a boy without fear, but he had felt the next thing to it at the sight of that face. He still had trouble getting his breath, and he sure would have enjoyed some company now.

Outside, the storm was 50 per cent louder and one hundred percent wetter. As soon as he left the protection of the house, the wind slammed into his face, so hard he felt as if he had eaten ice cream too fast.

He started across the yard, trying to reach the oak tree.

But the wind
blew him
like a sailboat
all
the
way
back
to
the
house.

He got down
on his hands and knees,
crawling across the wet, muddy yard
until
he came
to the cottage.

"Hey, open up!" he yelled. "It's me—Marco!"

"*Who?*" the wind roared. "*Who-o-o?*"

He pounded on the door, yelling. At least he thought he was yelling. He could hear nothing but that stupid, nosey wind.

The next thing he knew, his hand slipped off
                                        the wet doorknob
                          and
                      here
                he
              was
            again
          sailing,
      back
    across
the yard,
the beam
of the flashlight
in his fist
whirling around
like a beacon.

This time, he ended up close to the hall window. He crawled forward, along the foundation of the house. There, before his eyes, in the light of the flash, were a number of bare footprints. But there, before his eyes, they gradually disappeared in the steady waterfall that came pouring from the roof of Shady Hall with a surprisingly loud splatter. The wind was dying down . . . the rain was letting up. . . . Hurricane Inez was moving on.

Marco noticed something small and shiny in the mud under the window, and picked it up. That was when he saw the snake.

Water moccasin!

Thick and brown, glistening with rain, it was coiled next to the wall, not five feet away, its tiny, red eyes glowing in the light of the flash.

Slowly, slowly, Marco stood and backed away, watching the snake . . . as it watched him. He came to the enclosed porch, opened the lattice door, and stepped inside, thinking as he took the first step, wait a minute, wait a minute. . . .

Too late! He felt a numbing shock on his left shoulder, immediately followed by a second shock on his right shoulder. He gasped as the bucket of water poured over him, and he sat with a thump on the floor.

Clang!

That was the frying pan, glancing off the bucket on his head.

Clang-a-bang-ker-plang!

That was the frying pan, hitting the floor.

Clunk-a-blunk-alunk!

That was the kettle landing and rolling around on the floor. A sound like sleet came from the falling tacks. And that steady, syrupy drip, drip, drip—that was the can of bright red paint.

Marco, you brainless Marco, the boy thought, you've set off the Prowler Trap!

"All right, hold it right there, you—you with the bucket on your head!"

Marco peeked out from under the edge of the bucket. Sheriff Sam Y. Gross, stood in the doorway with a very power-ful flashlight in one hand, and his huge revolver in the other —AND a mighty dangerous look on his long, brown face.

"Why, it's Marco!" Mr. Cooper exclaimed.

"It sure is!" Eugene Gerard agreed.

"Huh, huh, huh!" Tolliver chuckled.

Marco wished with all his heart, that he was at the North Pole, wrestling a polar bear—or at the South Pole, counting penguins.

"What's going on out there?" Miss Hazel demanded from the door to the porch.

"Yeah!" Lily shouted. "Marco Fennerty, get up off that

floor and take that silly bucket off your head!"

"*Merr-ow!*"

It could not be worse. Never in a hundred, million, billion years could anything be worse. Marco stood up, blinking in the light of the flash, smiling shyly, removing the bucket. Then he felt the little thing he had picked up outside the hall window. It was, he saw, a harmonica.

He took a deep breath, then blew into it.

Tolliver raised his golden head, and gave the best howl that had ever come out of his red and black jaws. It rose up into the night, and seemed to make Hurricane Inez move off even faster.

"Anyway," Marco told them, "now we know what makes Tolliver howl."

12

LOST IN BIG GREEN SWAMP

Marco awoke the next morning to the whack of axes. Broken branches and whole uprooted trees lay in a great tangle around Shady Hall, and men were chopping to clear the road out front.

Marco and Lily ate a quick breakfast, then went to get Eugene Gerard and Tolliver. They wanted to bring Curious Cat, but he had other things to do.

"Be careful, children," Miss Hazel called after them, "and be back for lunch!"

The three friends followed the dog down to the bank of Bayou Terrebonne. Two pirogues were tied to a wooden pier there. The single paddle in each dugout canoe was floating in the water that nearly filled both boats.

The water in the bayou had fallen to its normal level, leaving behind a generous amount of black mud, in which could be seen the tiny tracks of animals heading back home. High overhead in the cloudless sky, gulls and other sea birds were flying south. The morning was beautiful, the air smelling like a fresh bedsheet.

"Well, Marco, how's the head?" Eugene Gerard asked.

Marco checked it carefully. "A little sore."

"I should think so," Lily said. "Brother!"

"But that was pretty smart of you to figure out what makes old Tolliver howl," Eugene Gerard told him. "The fella must have dropped the harmonica when you caught him at the window."

"The sheriff sure got to Shady Hall fast," Marco said.

"He must have been passing by," Lily answered. "We couldn't call him. We couldn't get Dr. Slade, either. We kept getting the busy signal."

"The storm must have knocked out the phone," Eugene Gerard said.

As the trio walked along the twisting bayou, leaving an impressive series of their own tracks in the mud, Marco and Lily told their friend the latest developments in the case.

"Two hundred thousand dollars!" Eugene Gerard exclaimed. "No wonder that fella is trying to scare everyone out of Shady Hall!"

"Marco, do you think Henri Cassatt's the one?" Lily asked. "Do you think he bashed Jim Danton in the head with a club?"

"The sheriff doesn't think so," Marco told her. "Have you ever seen Henri Cassatt?" he asked Eugene Gerard.

"No, not up close."

"Why'd you want to know that?" Lily asked. "Oh, the face!"

The only sound was the smacking of their feet in the sticky mud. Probably, Marco thought, his cousin and Eugene Gerard were thinking about the horrible face he had described. He saw it again in his mind's eye. Gungah!

Up ahead, they heard roosters crowing, hens clucking, dogs barking. They rounded a turn in the bayou and there was a low steel bridge. Next to it was a little wooden shack.

Marco squared his shoulders. "Come on."

"Right behind you," Lily replied.

"This is it," Eugene Gerard added.

They walked across the yard, past the clucking hens, and

barking dogs, Tolliver sniffing the dogs, they sniffing him. A rooster perched in a nearby tree cleared his throat, flapped his wings, and gave a hearty crow. The door of the shack opened, and a man stepped out on the porch.

He looked like a fullback. He was not very tall, but he was very wide. He appeared to be wearing shoulder pads under his shirt, but Marco knew it was muscle from opening and closing the bridge. The man was dressed in blue work pants and work shirt, both of which had seen a mess of work—and a mess of washing.

He had a face like an old brick—red, square, and deeply lined. It was not the face Marco had seen at the window. The man stood with his hands on his hips, staring down at the trio. A white rooster was perched on one shoulder.

"What for you come here, eh?" the man asked. "You reckon it's Halloween and you trick-or-treating?"

"No, sir," Marco answered. "We're—"

"You sell cookies for them Boy Scout and Girl Scout?"

"No, sir," Marco said. "We're from Shady Hall—"

"Shady Hall, eh? I don't hear about y'all there, me."

Marco introduced himself, his cousin, and Eugene Gerard, explaining to the bridge tender that they wanted to ask him a few questions.

"Ask all them question you want," Henri Cassatt replied. "I got plenty time, me."

Marco glanced at his cousin and Eugene Gerard.

"Well, go ahead," Lily told him. But the boy, for the moment, could not think of a good question to start with.

"Y'all want to come in? Come on. But take off them shoe. I just make the whole place clean."

The three climbed the wooden steps to the porch, where they removed their muddy shoes. Mr. Cassatt was barefooted, Marco noticed, and he had big feet.

"What's the matter with them feet?"

"Nothing, sir," the boy replied.

The bridge tender waved his visitors inside. The shack had one room, most of which was taken up by a big bed. Lying on it were three cats, a dog, and a pair of raccoons.

Marco glanced around the room, noticing that it was very clean. On a table in the back was a small radio, but that was Henri Cassatt's only link with the rest of the world. How, the boy wondered, could anyone live without books?

"What you look for?"

"I was just surprised to see no books, or magazines, or newspapers," Marco replied. "This must be a lonely life."

"I don't read, not too well, no," Mr. Cassatt replied. "But I'm not lonely, me. Them animal keep me all the company I want. I talk to them and they listen good. When they get in the fight, I fuss at them and they stop right now—oh, yeah!"

Lily nodded toward the iron stove in the corner. Leaning against it was a long wooden club.

Marco swallowed. "Mr. Cassatt, what's the club for?"

"For them snake on the bridge."

The bridge tender sat on the edge of the bed, taking one of the raccoons into his lap.

"That devil, he's the bestest of the whole bunch. His name is Sparkplug, but I call him 'Red.' You talk about smart! Them boat come by at night when I'm asleep, and he jump on me and wake me up, that devil, so I go open the bridge."

Henri Cassatt glanced up at them. His eyes were very blue in his red face. "What are them thing you want to know?"

"We wanted to ask you about Jim Danton," Eugene Gerard told him.

The bridge tender stroked the raccoon. "He come by all the time, Jim."

"Was he a friend of yours?" Lily asked.

"Bestest friend a man can have, yeah. But then Jim, Jim, he drown, Jim." Henri Cassatt shook his head. He seemed to be deeply moved.

"Mr. Cassatt," Marco said softly, "there's a story going around that you didn't come to the funeral because you were mad at Jim Danton."

The bridge tender glared—not at the boy, but at the story. "I can't come," he replied. "I can't leave that bridge."

"You couldn't get off even to go to a funeral?" Marco asked.

"I don't leave that bridge in twenty year, me," Mr. Cassatt answered with some pride. "I get the vacation every year, but I don't take it, no. The city council can't get the man to take my place, and I don't like to leave them animal."

"But why couldn't you have taken a couple of hours to go to the funeral?" Lily asked.

"The mayor get the man to watch the bridge for me so I can go, but then he has the car wreck and break his arm, so I have to stay here sure enough."

"Mr. Cassatt," Eugene Gerard said, "there's another story that you thought Mr. Danton was going to leave you some money in his will."

"He leave me no money in the will, Jim."

Marco glanced at Lily and Eugene Gerard, then turned back to the bridge tender. "Were you expecting some, sir?" he asked.

"Me? No."

"Oh!"

"You know what that man do?" Mr. Cassatt asked. "About a week, two week, before he sail to that bay that time, he come by here, Jim, and he give me a check for five thousand dollar to pay off the rest of the house—oh, yeah! He been one fine man, Jim."

"He sure was," Marco agreed. "Thank you, Mr. Cassatt, we'd better be going."

The bridge tender walked the three to the door. The raccoon was draped over one shoulder.

"Been nice time to see y'all, kids," he told them as they were putting on their shoes. "Come back visit me again. You find that man what's telling all them story, you let Henri know. I take him and I break his neck for him, yeah!"

At the bend in the bayou the trio turned to wave good-by. Henri Cassatt waved back with both arms.

"Do you believe him?" Lily asked her cousin. "And you'd better say 'yes,' " she warned.

"I do."

"So do I," Eugene Gerard said.

"Me, too," Lily declared.

She and Marco left Eugene Gerard at the cottage with Tolliver and after removing their shoes again, entered Shady Hall. Marco went into the study, thinking about a mess of things but mainly in terms of lunch. The long hike down and back through the mud had given him an appetite.

The grandfather clock in the hall struck twelve noon. Half of Friday gone, the boy thought, and he wasn't about to solve the mystery of Shady Hall—wasn't even close. He walked slowly up and down the room, the solemn clock ticks keeping time with his steps.

Then a flashing on the wall caught his eye. It came through the window from the direction of Bayou Terrebonne. He peered out the window, but could see nothing.

"What're you looking at?" Lily asked, coming into the room. She joined Marco at the window. The flashing came again from a clump of trees along the bayou.

"Maybe somebody's trying to signal us," she suggested.

"*Come back visit me again. You find that man what's telling all them story,*" the bridge tender told them.

"I don't believe so," he replied. "It's more like—yeah! Somebody's watching Shady Hall. That must be the sun flashing on his glasses. Come on!"

Like a pair of Indians, the boy and his cousin slipped out of the study door and sneaked down to the bank. But they weren't sneaky enough. There came to their ears the explosive roar of an outboard motor. By the time the two had reached the bank, the motorboat—with its single occupant crouched forward—was racing up the bayou, leaving a wide "V" of green water in its wake.

Marco untied one of the pirogues.

"Get in the boat," he told Lily. "You bail—I'll paddle."

She climbed in and sat down in the water, exclaiming, "Yuch!"

The pirogue had a way of wobbling. Marco paddled on one side, then on the other, and the dugout went rocking forward as Lily scooped the water out with her hands, making a face.

The bayou was getting narrower. Oaks on both sides stretched out their branches across the water to each other, and Spanish moss drooped from one branch to the next like an old torn tent. The pirogue passed the gleaming white skull of a cow stuck on a wooden post, and a rusty metal sign nailed to a tree. The sign once had said—and still did, if you looked closely enough:

Big Green Swamp
DANGER

Ahead was a great wall of leaves that seemed to end the stream; but, as the pirogue came to it, the channel of the bayou appeared to the left. Marco paddled on until the dugout came to a huge pond with cypresses sticking up out of the

It seemed to Marco as he dragged the dugout along that he and Lily had entered another world.

water, like scrawny Christmas trees.

Perhaps Marco's arms were getting tired, but it seemed to him that the water here was thicker and more difficult to move the boat through. The air was heavy with the odor of rotting vegetation and a wild smell of—maybe foxes, maybe bobcats, maybe panthers!

An alligator rose up like a black log, like a U-boat. He took a good look at the two people in the pirogue with his crafty red eyes, then sank like a rock, leaving a trail of bubbles and a series of rings in the water.

Big Green Swamp had a terrible stillness. All around the trees were reflected in the bayou in a very spooky manner. It seemed to Marco, as he dragged the dugout along with the dripping paddle, that he and Lily had entered another world where up was down, and down was up.

"Low bridge," the boy warned. The two ducked as the pirogue passed under a mossy log—and over its reflection in the green mirror of still water.

Once again, a wall of leaves appeared to close off the bayou. But, as before, just when the pirogue reached the leaves, the channel appeared—this time to the right. Once more, the bayou broadened to a big pond. This one was filled with water lilies, and the plopping bubbles of marsh gas that exploded on the surface.

"Phew!" Lily exclaimed. "Let's get out of here!"

Marco dug the paddle into the bubbling water, but the pirogue didn't seem to want to go anywhere. His arms were *some* tired.

"Getting tired?" Lily asked.

"Nah!"

"Yes, you are. Give me that paddle."

He did as he was told. Lily paddled strongly. They came to a gloomy forest, the branches of the trees meeting overhead.

The sunlight that filtered down through the leaves and moss was green and dim.

"Marco, listen!"

There was only that terrible stillness.

"What happened to the outboard?" Lily asked. "You think that guy's hiding somewhere, watching us?"

"Nah!"

But he did feel eyes. An armadillo was studying them from a clump of palmetto. Farther down the bank, a muskrat was sitting upright like a squirrel, watching them as he munched on a clam. And high overhead a buzzard, with just one thing on its evil little mind, circled like a black "T."

"Let's get out of this awful place," Lily urged.

"I'm with you," Marco agreed.

The trouble was that he had no idea how. They had taken so many twists, and so many turns in the watery jungle that all the passages, all the ponds, all the mossy oaks and cypresses looked alike.

Lily paddled until she was tired, then Marco took over. And then, when he couldn't drag the paddle through the thick water any more, she took it back from him.

"Know something?" she asked. "We're lost."

"Nah."

"Yes, we are, Marco, and you know it. Wish we'd had time for lunch before we started."

The bayou spread out into another big pond. Flies and other unidentified swampland insects zipped around, their wings glowing, as if on fire when they hit the golden shafts of light from the afternoon sun. The light was slanting sharply— it was getting late.

As they moved across the pond, Marco, who was paddling once more, swallowed hard. He sure could use a drink of water—but not *that* water. He glanced up. Sitting on the limb of a dead tree, its cruel eyes glinting from its pink, bare, ugly head, was the buzzard—or at least *a* buzzard. It sat there, watching them patiently.

"Marco, what're we gonna do?"

"Gonna get out of here."

"How?"

The boy checked the sunlight. In another few hours it would be dark. Already the shadows of the trees were inching across the water, and only the topmost branches were still in the sun's rays. There were better places to spend the night than in Big Green Swamp.

"I asked you how?" Lily reminded him.

"I'll show you how," he answered. "We want to go south —right?"

"Right, but how can we know what way is south? And don't give me that stuff about moss growing on the north side of trees. This stupid moss grows all *over* the trees."

"Listen," he told her, "when you face north, west is on your left side and east is on your right. And south is behind you."

"So which way's north?"

"We know that way is west," he said, pointing with the paddle, "because the sun sets in the west."

"Don't talk about the sun setting!"

"So we swing the old boat around, so that the west is on our left," he said, paddling rapidly, "and the east is on our right. That means we're facing north."

"And south is behind us!" Lily exclaimed. "Oh, boy, Marco, let's get moving!"

"Set course for zero-niner-zero. All engines ahead at flank speed!"

He dug the paddle into the bayou and pulled the pirogue through the swirling water. He soon saw, however, that to

steer directly south was impossible. Things kept getting in the
way, and the passages weren't always where you wanted them
to be. Again and again, he had to stop and get his bearings
from the setting sun.

A shadow passed overhead, and the buzzard settled down
on a cypress knee, watching them as they came up. There was
a whine, and Marco slapped at a mosquito. The bugs would
be out in force before long. His arms were getting tired again.

"Marco, I'm scared. Aren't you?"

"Nah!"

"I bet. What if we have to spend the night here?"

"We're not going to."

"Pretty soon it'll be dark, and you won't know which way
the sun set, with all the turning around we have to do," she
said.

"Don't worry."

"If you don't mind, I'll worry."

Marco dug the paddle into the water, with arms that felt
as if they were made of lead. The bayou seemed to be full of
molasses and it was getting dimmer by the minute. The buzzard sailed overhead, and took up a new lookout post. The
mosquitoes began to appear in singing squadrons. He couldn't
paddle another stroke.

"Give me that thing," Lily said. "Oh, what's the use?
We'd be better off saving our strength to fight the bugs."

"Just let me rest a minute," Marco told her.

Hot blisters had formed on both palms, and his fingers
were so stiff, that his hands felt like iron claws. Bats came zig-
zagging through the air, gobbling bugs. An owl hooted, and,
somewhere off to their left, an animal of some kind screamed.

Marco picked up the paddle and resumed his struggle
with the bayou. One by one, the blisters popped, but he kept
paddling. The light was quite dim. He saw the growing fear

in Lily's face, and hoped she could see nothing in his, but the determined smile. That animal screamed again, and the buzzard passed overhead.

For the perhaps hundredth time, a bank of dark leaves seemed to block the bayou, then parted, revealing a passage. It led out onto still another pond. Marco doubted that, in their condition, it would be possible for them to live through a night in Big Green Swamp. He recalled Tad Payne's words: "No telling how many nosy kids have gone in there and never come out."

13

"GET OUT OF THIS HOUSE"

Marco glanced at Lily. She gave him a smile that looked as stiff as his own set grin felt. To pull up the muscles of your face and keep them there burned up a certain amount of energy, something he had in short supply. But soon it would be dark, and he wouldn't have to show her his phony grin—or any kind of face at all.

The crickets were singing/ringing, and then that chorus of 7,500 frogs joined in.

"I could do without those stupid frogs," Marco muttered.

"Listen," Lily told him. "The baby frog is saying, 'Can I go, can I go, can I go?' and the momma frog is saying, 'Ask your daddy, ask your daddy, ask your daddy.' And the poppa frog is saying, 'No! No! No!'"

"*Hmm*," Marco breathed, dragging the stupid paddle through the stupid, stubborn water. He thought, it was Wednesday, just two days ago, that he had asked his father about the trip to Shady Hall, "Can I go, can I go, can I go?" If Sergeant Fennerty had said, "No, no, no!," an eleven-year-old boy without fear would not be lost with his cousin in Big Green Swamp today—almost tonight.

From somewhere up ahead came a cry. It could have come from an owl or a bobcat, or it could have come from a panther. But it wasn't from any of these.

Gradually, the cry became clear. "Lily, Marco, where are you?"

"That's Eugene Gerard!" Lily exclaimed. "Here we are! she shouted. "Over here!"

Yelling back and forth, they found each other minutes later. Eugene Gerard was in the other pirogue.

"I'm glad to see you," Marco told him, shaking hands.

"Likewise," Lily said, shaking his other hand.

"How'd you know we were here?" Marco asked.

"I just naturally looked out my window and saw Curious Cat go barrelling down to the bayou," Eugene Gerard replied. "Then I saw you two going up the bayou at a somewhat slower rate of speed. And, when you didn't come back, I started to get somewhat worried."

"Where's Curious Cat now?" Marco asked.

"Don't know," Eugene Gerard answered. "But, come on, it'll be dark in a half-hour, and then we'll never get out of this place!"

"Aunt Hazel will be worried to death," Lily said. She and Marco transferred, wobbling, to the other pirogue. Marco brought his paddle, and helped Eugene Gerard propel the dugout through the noisy, shadowy swamp. Two guys working paddles sure made a difference. They left the other boat adrift.

"Children, where have you been?" Miss Hazel demanded when Marco and his cousin returned to Shady Hall. "Y'all had me worried sick!"

"I was giving Lily a pirogue ride on the bayou," the boy answered truthfully enough—just enough.

"How nice," Miss Hazel said. "But next time let me know before you go, and don't stay so long."

Next time, Marco thought. *Gungah!* As far as he was concerned, there would never be a next time in Big Green Swamp.

"What's for supper?" Lily asked.

Red beans and rice, one of Marco's favorite dishes—and apparently one his cousin's, too, from the way she dug in. She and her great-aunt had cooked the meal before the hurricane hit. Since Shady Hall was still without gas and lights, they had to eat their supper cold, but it tasted great. And candlelight was always nice.

"You missed Dr. Slade and Mr. Boudier," Miss Hazel remarked as the three were doing the dishes by the light of a lantern in the kitchen.

"When were they here?" Marco asked.

"Dr. Slade came a little after lunch to see how we had made out in the storm," she told him. "Mr. Boudier was here, oh, about two hours ago, I reckon, with some papers for me to sign."

"What kind of papers?" Marco asked.

"Receipts for some checks I've received from my daddy's trust fund, she replied. "Why, Marco?"

"Just wondering."

"Why did you want to know when they were here?" she asked.

"Just wondering. Miss Hazel, where's Curious Cat?"

"I don't know. I declare, I don't. I haven't seen him since around noon. I keep hearing him, but I can't find him."

"*Merr-ow.*"

The cry was faint. It seemed to be close by, and yet, at the same time, it sounded as if it came from far, far away. Miss Danton, her grandniece, and Marco searched the house—opening closets, cupboards, front doors, back doors. But Curious Cat did not appear.

"*Merr-ow.*"

"Curious Cat, where are you?" Marco called. "Here, Curious, Curious, Curious Cat!"

"*Merr-ow.*"

The cry seemed to come from all over Shady Hall.

"He'll be okay," Lily remarked. "I'm tired. I believe I'll go to bed."

"Excellent idea," her great aunt replied. "Excellent! Come on, Marco. Everything's locked and barred. We'll make a fresh start in the morning."

He really should do some figuring about things, the boy thought as he wearily climbed the stairs. But the truth of the matter was that the only things he could think about right now were his aching arms—to say nothing of his painful shoulders, chest, and back.

Once in his room, he automatically put on his pajamas, blew out the candle, crawled into bed, pulled up the covers . . . and almost immediately was asleep.

Some time later he awoke with a vague, uneasy feeling as if somebody or something was calling him. Downstairs, the grumpy grandfather clock struck the half-hour of some hour or other. The musty, muddy smell of Bayou Terror was strong.

Abruptly, Marco sat up. A shaft of moonlight slanted in through the window, resting easily on the foot of the bed. He heard something. It was that strange, breathing noise that had come to his ears so many times in Shady Hall, but, this time, it was much louder. It seemed to come right into his left ear.

The boy jumped out of bed and grabbed his flashlight. The slender beam showed him something he hadn't noticed before—a small hole by the side of the bed, a round, neat hole about the size of a quarter. The breathing sound—and the smell of Bayou Terror—came from the hole.

Marco crouched, listening. . . .

He heard a creak, a groan—the noises of old timbers settling down for still another night in the long, sad history of Shady Hall.

"*Merr-ow!*"

The cry of Curious Cat came clearly through the hole.

There was a pause and then the boy heard a hoarse voice say, "Hazel Danton! Hazel Danton! Get out of this house! This house is cursed!"

Marco jerked back, as if punched in the ear. Almost at once, there came through the little hole a wild scream—the scream of Curious Cat in great pain.

The boy went pounding down the steps to the first floor, following the beam of his flashlight.

As he ran, the hoarse words came back to him. The voice hadn't said, "*that* house" it had said, "*this* house," which meant the guy had spoken from inside Shady Hall—and might still be here!

Marco was running down the stairs so fast, however, that he couldn't stop until he hit bottom. He flashed the light around, but saw no one or nothing.

"*Merr-ow!*"

Curious Cat came strolling into the hall from the kitchen. He was covered with cobwebs, and, sticking to his black fur, were three or four moths—all quite dead.

The boy went into the kitchen. The back door was wide open.

"I'm right certain I locked that door," Miss Hazel declared, entering the room. Her voice was steady, but her hand was not, and the fluttering flame of the candle she held showed the fear in her white face.

"Wasn't that voice awful?" her grandniece asked, following her into the kitchen.

Marco shut the back door and locked it.

"Anyway, the guy's gone now," the boy said. "Miss Hazel, there's a little hole in the wall of my room by the bed. What's it for?"

"All the bedrooms have them," she replied. "Sometime

toward the end of the nineteenth century, Shady Hall was equipped with a system of speaking tubes. They go from all the bedrooms to the kitchen, here . . ."

She walked over to the stove and held out her candle. In the wall, to the right of the stove, was a hole similar to the one in Marco's bedroom.

"The system was installed so we Dantons could order breakfast or whatever, and summon servants, and all like that."

"That's why Shady Hall sometimes has that funny breathing noise," the boy said. "A breeze or draft comes through the house and makes the hissing sound in the tubes."

"So that's it!"

"Miss Hazel, has Tad Payne ever been in Shady Hall?"

"Years ago, yes. Why?"

"Then he could know about the speaking tubes."

"I expect so, but they're not uncommon in old houses."

"Why did you want to know about Tad Payne especially?" Lily asked.

"I wasn't asking about him especially," Marco replied. "The guy we're looking for has to know this place pretty well. And I sort of got the idea that Mr. Payne hasn't been exactly welcome in Shady Hall for quite some time. Miss Hazel, how about Henri Cassatt?"

"Oh, yes. Before he became the bridge tender, about twenty years ago, Henri used to come here right much."

"Marco!" Lily exclaimed accusingly. "You said you believed him!"

"Sure," the boy agreed. "But he's still a suspect, And I guess he could get rid of that Cajun accent for just a couple of sentences."

"What about Dr. Slade?" Lily demanded. "What about Mr. Boudier?"

"Lily, we *know* they've been here a mess of times," Marco told her.

"Why did Curious Cat scream like that?" she asked.

"I guess the guy stepped on his tail in the dark," the boy replied. "I don't believe he did it on purpose."

"I don't know about that," Lily told him.

"Well, children, we've had enough excitement for one night," Miss Danton said. "Let's get some sleep, and have an early start at searching in the morning."

This time, it took Marco longer to go to sleep . . . but not much. Something Henri Cassatt had said—what was it? Something about tricks. Somebody playing a trick on somebody, something like that. He was just about to remember when sleep came down like a dark curtain.

14

A KNOCK AT THE DOOR

"I didn't sleep a wink," Lily told her great aunt and Marco at breakfast the next morning. "Not a wink! I kept hearing that awful voice!"

The boy poured milk over his corn flakes. "You know," he said, "I believe the way to solve this case is with those letters. A guy can maybe change his voice, but he can't change his handwriting."

"So what are we going to do?"

"Not *we*, Miss Priss," her great aunt broke in. "You're staying here with me. We've got us a job of work right here at Shady Hall, cleaning up the mess from Hurricane Inez."

"Aunt Hazel!" Lily exclaimed in protest. "Wish I was a boy," she said, almost to herself. "Okay, Marco, what are *you* going to do?"

"Going to go see the sheriff and ask him to take me around to everybody and have them write 'Get out of that house,' and 'That house is cursed.' Then compare their writing with the writing in the letters."

"What if the people won't do it?"

"That," the boy replied, "would appear mighty suspicious. *Mighty* suspicious."

He borrowed Eugene Gerard's bike again and rode into town. New Paris looked like an army camp, with tents pitched all around the courthouse square. A captain or general was giving commands over a bullhorn; sergeants, with no need of such artificial equipment, were shouting orders to privates. Marco parked the bike and went up to the sheriff's office.

"You again," Deputy Hornbrook commented, opening the door. "You sure pick the times, don't you? We're up to our ears. Well, you can't see the sheriff. He's out."

A hand clamped down on Marco's shoulder from behind him.

"Howdy, pard," Sheriff Gross said, coming in. "How we doing on the Shady Hall Case?"

He brought Marco into his office, shut the door, and slumped down in his chair under the American Flag and the picture of Wyatt Earp. He looked tired, and appeared to have added another dozen or so lines in his face.

The boy told him all that had taken place—surprised in the telling that so much had happened—since they had last seen each other at the Prowler Trap that night of the hurricane. Then he described his plan of getting the handwriting specimens.

"Good idea," Sheriff Gross replied, taking a pad of paper and a pen from his desk. "Fine idea. Come on, pard, saddle up. Hold it down, Jasper."

Deputy Hornbrook stuck up a hand with the thumb and first finger, forming a circle.

First, the sheriff and Marco went to see Tad Payne.

The mechanic cocked his head at the boy and asked the law man, "New deputy?"

The sheriff ignored the question. "Mr. Payne," he said, "would you have any objection to giving us a specimen of your handwriting?"

"Maybe I would and maybe I wouldn't," the mechanic replied. "What's the big idea?"

As briefly as possible, the sheriff told him about the letters. Mr. Payne cracked his greasy knuckles. "And you think I'm the one who wrote them," he said.

"Not necessarily," the sheriff replied.

"Was this *his* idea?" the mechanic asked, cocking his head at Marco.

The sheriff nodded. "Yup."

"All right, let's get this silly game over with. What do you want me to write?"

" 'Get out of that house,' and 'That house is cursed.' "

Taking the pen in his greasy right hand, Mr. Payne wrote rapidly on the pad. There was a smudge on the sheet. He had written, "That kid is too smart for his own good."

The sheriff's voice was stern: "Come on now, Mr. Payne."

The mechanic shrugged and wrote the two sentences as directed.

Next, the sheriff and Marco went to see Antoine Boudier, Attorney at Law. He was sitting at his desk as before, asleep as before, and with the same rather clean handkerchief covering the top of his big, bald head. He awoke cranky, as before.

"What do *you* know for the good of your country?" he demanded of Marco, as before.

"Mr. Boudier," the sheriff asked, "do you have any objection to giving us a specimen of your handwriting?"

The lawyer looked up with a mocking smile. "Are you sure of your legal grounds, Sheriff?"

"I'm asking you, Mr. Boudier."

"This is in connection with all the goings-on at Shady Hall, I expect."

The light flashed on Antoine Boudier's glasses as he glanced up sharply. "And don't ask me how I would know that?" he added. "It's quite obvious y'all are working on a case together, and what else could it be?"

He took the pad, pushed back the top sheet with his rather fat left hand, and picked up his own pen out of its holder with his rather fat right hand.

"Fire away!" He wrote down the sentences as the sheriff dictated them.

The lawman and Marco found Dr. Slade in the Magnolia Drug Store, having a cup of coffee at the lunch counter. He greeted them with a gleaming smile.

"Dr. Slade, would you have any objection to giving us a specimen of your handwriting?" the sheriff asked.

"None whatever." The doctor reached his right hand into his pocket and took out a gold fountain pen. "How about 'The quick brown fox jumped over the lazy dog?' " he asked.

"We'd like you to write, 'Get out of that house,' and 'That house is cursed,' " the sheriff told him.

Dr. Slade stopped smiling. "What *is* this?" he demanded. The lawman told him about the letters Miss Danton had received.

"And I'm a suspect."

Dr. Slade glared from Sheriff Gross to Marco and back again. Then he shrugged, smiling. "You know, they say the only person who can read a doctor's handwriting is a druggist, but here goes. Let me have those two lines again."

Last on the list was Henri Cassatt. The lawman and Marco put the bike in the trunk of the patrol car, then drove out to the Bayou Terrebonne bridge.

"Sheriff," the boy asked, "what'll happen to the guy that's doing all this when we catch him?"

"You mean his punishment? I don't rightly know, pard. I'll have to check the penal law. This is not a common crime, let me tell you. I've served eight terms as sheriff of Napoleon Parish—up for reelection this November coming, as I might have mentioned—and I've never come across anything like this."

"I see."

"There might be several different types of crime involved here. They might come under the general heading of 'malicious mischief.'"

Mischief, the boy thought. Tricks!

"The hombre might be convicted of extortion—in this case getting money by terrorizing his victim, Miss Danton. Anyway, I reckon it's safe enough to say that it's not so much the legal punishment he would suffer as the punishment of being exposed to everyone in New Paris as the hombre who has pulled all these tricks."

Tricks, Marco thought. Trick-or-treating . . .

The radio sputtered as if it had been dropped into a pot of boiling grease.

"Car One, Car One, do you read me?"

The sheriff picked up the microphone: "Coming in loud and clear, Jasper."

"Car one, Car One, do you read me?"

The sheriff's tired eyes met Marco's. "Jasper has to have everything just so," he explained. "Car One," he said into the mike. "We read you."

"Car One, this is Deputy Hornbrook at Headquarters."

"Car One thought so," the lawman replied. "What's the problem, Jasper?"

"Sheriff, the Red Cross is bringing food and clothes for the refugees in by the truckload. What'll I do with it all?"

"Put it in the jail, Jasper. I'll be back soon. Ten-four?"

"Roger. I'll hold things down till you get here. Over and out."

The patrol car came to the bridge and the little shack beside it. Henri Cassatt walked out on the porch, with the rooster perched on his shoulder as if it had never left. A big white smile cracked the brick-red of the bridge tender's face.

"Hi, Marco! You come back, eh? Good! Hi, Sam! Come in, y'all, and pass pleasure."

"We're here on official business, Henri," the lawman told him, climbing the stairs to the porch.

The bridge tender was puzzled. "Sure enough?"

"Henri, we'd like you to give us a specimen of your handwriting," Sheriff Gross said. "We want you to write a couple of sentences for us."

"What for, eh?"

The lawman told him. Henri Cassatt listened carefully, saying nothing.

"Will you do that, Henri?"

"I don't reckon so, me."

"Henri, it would be better for you if you did," the sheriff pointed out. "All we're asking you to do is write, 'Get out of that house,' and, 'That house is cursed.' "

Some time ago, the bridge tender had stopped smiling. "I don't write them thing—you hear? Now, Sheriff Gross, and you, kid, git off the porch and plum off the land!"

"Saddle up, pard," the lawman told Marco. "We'll come back when he has simmered down a bit."

The two drove in silence back to Shady Hall.

"I don't believe he's the one," Marco said as they were getting the bike out of the trunk.

"Me, neither," the lawman replied. "I'll see you, pard."

"See you, Sheriff."

"Marco," Miss Hazel greeted him, "Mr. Cooper had to go to Vicksburg to report on the hurricane damage along Bayou Terrebonne. Why don't we ask Eugene Gerard over for supper? We can have hamburgers on the grill."

"Hamburgers on the grill!" Lily exclaimed.

It should have been a pleasant evening, but Marco was depressed from the session with Henri Cassatt, and confused by the bridge tender's attitude. Also, none of the handwriting specimens the sheriff and he had collected today looked at all like the writing in the letters.

Miss Hazel, Lily, Eugene Gerard, and he were all sitting in the study by candlelight, talking things over, as the grandfather clock in the hall tolled the quarter-hours . . . the half-hours . . . the hours. Eleven o'clock!

"But, Marco, why couldn't the bad guy change his handwriting the same way he could change his voice?" Lily asked. "Wouldn't it be just as easy?"

"I don't believe so. There'd be certain ways of forming the capitals and other letters that would be bound to slip out."

"Maybe they could disguise their writing if they wrote real slow and concentrated on each letter," Eugene Gerard suggested.

"Right man. They all made a humbug about giving us the specimens. But, when they actually started writing, they just zipped them off—everyone, that is, but Henri Cassatt."

Lily groaned.

Marco felt the same way. The clock struck the quarter-hour. Another forty-five minutes and it would be Sunday, his last day at Shady Hall. There was so much to mull over—and do. The boy rubbed his head, saying to himself, "Think, brain. Think!"

"Maybe it's somebody else who's writing the letters and all like that," Miss Hazel suggested.

"Maybe," Marco replied miserably.

"*Merr-ow!*"

Curious Cat was back in his lofty lair on the bookshelf. His long black tail was twitching nervously, as it had the night of the hurricane.

The familiar—and no longer spooky—sigh came through Shady Hall. Then there came another sound, so soft and secretive it might not have been a sound at all, until another came after it slightly louder—a tapping.

"Something's at the door!" Miss Danton exclaimed.

The tapping came a third time, just a bit louder.

"It sounds like it's coming from the hall," Marco told them, pulling out his flashlight. He and Eugene Gerard ran out into the hall, as the tapping came again.

"It's coming from the door to the tunnel!" Marco yelled.

"Don't let it in!" Miss Danton screamed.

The heavy wooden door wasn't barred! In the light of the flash, the boys saw the door begin to open, slowly.

"Don't let it in!" Miss Hazel screamed again.

The boys charged the door, throwing all their weight against it. Marco grabbed the thick iron bar and slammed it home with a grating thud.

A knock sounded in their ears, inches away, another, another—each louder than before. They stood back from the door, hearing the knocks echo through Shady Hall.

Then all was silence.

"Maybe it has gone away," Miss Danton whispered. "But how did it get down there in the first place?"

She and Lily stood, hugging each other, in the hall behind the boys.

The knocking came again. Now it was so loud and fast that it sounded like thunder. The door shook under the blows, and they could hear a splintering. A crack appeared in the wood.

"No human fist could hit a door that hard," Marco shouted into his friend's ear.

"Wish old Tolliver was here," Eugene Gerard yelled back.

Lily and her great aunt screamed—and screamed again,

as the crashing knocks continued in violence. Marco tightened his stomach muscles, thinking TNT, TNT. "Who's there?" he shouted. "What do you want?" He did not expect an answer, but didn't want to scream hysterically—and he had to get rid of the pressure in his chest.

"Shut up!" Eugene Gerard yelled at the door. "Leave us alone!"

The crashes continued for another ten seconds or so, then stopped. The echoes chased each other through the dark rooms of Shady Hall, and then they died out, too. There was only the noise of the grumpy grandfather clock as it tolled the half-hour, and the sighing sound of four people letting out their breath.

"It's gone," Miss Danton whispered. "But maybe not!"

"It's gone, don't worry," Marco told her. "Miss Hazel, you and Lily lock yourselves in the study. Come on, pal."

The two boys waited until they heard the click of the study door. Then, for a moment, they looked at each other in the light of the flash. And then, while Marco squared his shoulders, Eugene Gerard slid the iron bar back and pulled the door open.

Marco shot the flashlight beam down the stairs. The cobweb curtains were badly torn. They wavered in the breeze that brought up the muddy, musty smell of Bayou Terror. The two boys started down the plank steps.

At the bottom, they saw a jagged hole in what had been the wall sealing up the tunnel. The bricks that had fallen out were all in a jumble on the muddy floor. Lying by the steps was the long pole with the hook on the end.

"Come on, pal," Marco said, stepping through the hole.

"I'm with you, pal," Eugene Gerard replied.

They followed the golden beam of the flash through the moldy brick tunnel until they came to another jagged hole in

Staring down at them, seeming to hang in the air, covered with cobwebs and several dead moths, was the horrible face.

the remains of another wall. They stepped through—and almost fell into Bayou Terror.

Marco swept the flash around, then stepped back with a gasp, almost knocking over his friend.

"That face!" Eugene Gerard exclaimed.

Staring down at them, seeming to hang in the air, covered with cobwebs and several dead moths, was the horrible inhuman face Marco had seen outside the hall window the night of the hurricane. Deathly white, black holes for eyes, tusks for teeth, it slowly turned in the breeze. It was like the face of a highwayman from the old days who had been caught, hanged, and had his head chopped off to dangle as a warning to others in his wicked business.

Marco made himself chuckle, made his hand reach for the horrible thing.

"Know what that is?" he asked.

"Yeah," Eugene Gerard breathed. "A Halloween mask."

15

THE LOCKED ROOM

Sunday. To Marco it had never been the beginning of the week, but the end. He was always a bit sad on Sunday, just as he was when he came to the final chapter of a book. On his last day at Shady Hall, he really felt down in the dumps. He was also annoyed at his brain, which just wouldn't work, no matter what he told it.

He sat in the study—after an early Mass and a late breakfast—with his cousin and Eugene Gerard, and with Curious Cat in his lap. Miss Danton was banging around in the kitchen.

The boy held the rubber Halloween mask, a silly-looking thing by day, even though it was so horrible by night.

"Why did the guy leave it?" Lily asked.

"Well, you can see it's torn," Marco told her. "I guess he caught it on the bush when he was coming out of the tunnel and just pulled it off and left it hanging there when he jumped in his boat to make his getaway."

"Probably the fella wanted to get rid of it anyway, since it would be powerful evidence against him if he was caught with it," Eugene Gerard added.

"Do you suppose he was wearing it to scare us?" Lily asked.

"No, I think it was mainly just to hide his face," Marco replied, stroking Curious Cat's silky black chin.

"In other words, we would recognize him." Lily hugged

herself, shivering. "But you don't think he was wearing it Friday when we caught him watching Shady Hall."

"No, I believe he was just wearing a big pair of sunglasses to hide his face some. He must have found out then that the wall sealing the tunnel had fallen down during the hurricane."

Lily tossed her hair back. "Those two rumbles we heard that night!" she exclaimed.

"Right," he said. "Bayou Terror must have been seeping through the walls for years, and then the high water from the storm finished off the job."

"Funny we didn't notice the hole when we came back from Big Green Swamp," Eugene Gerard remarked. "Of course it was dark by then, and the pier is a little north of the tunnel."

"Curious Cat must have found the tunnel open after he followed us down to the bank," Marco said. "He went in to investigate, and then couldn't get out."

"Why not?" Lily asked.

"Probably the water of Bayou Terror was blocking it," he answered. "The tide was coming in—say, that's one of the reasons we had so much trouble paddling, we were going against the tide!"

"So you people couldn't find Curious Cat Friday night because he was in the cellar," Eugene Gerard said.

"Right," Marco agreed. "Then when the guy came through the tunnel later that night, Curious Cat came in the house with him."

"So that's how the guy got in!" Lily exclaimed. "I knew I'd seen Aunt Hazel lock the back door. But, wait a second, Marco. The tunnel door has a bolt. You can't open it from the inside."

"Someone could have slipped the bolt earlier," the boy

replied. "But my guess is that a brainless lad named Marco Fennerty, Junior, forgot to lock it after he went down there the night before."

He hauled off and gave himself a good one.

"Hey!" Lily exclaimed. "Don't do that. We need you thinking straight."

"So the fella slips into the kitchen," Eugene Gerard said, "delivers his little pep talk into the speaking tube, steps on Curious Cat's tail in the dark, and exits out the back door."

"Then he comes back through the tunnel last night and tries to get into the house the same way," Lily went on.

"I don't believe he wanted to get in last night," Marco told her. "If he had, he wouldn't have knocked first, letting us know he was there."

Lily tossed her hair back. "Well, what was his idea?"

"Same as it's been all along," the boy replied. "To scare everyone out of the house so he can search it and find the pile of money before the National Trust people start to fix up Shady Hall."

"At which time the workers would probably come across the loot," Eugene Gerard added.

"So he wasn't trying to get in, or break the door down," Lily said. "I guess that's why he left when he did, because he saw he *was* breaking it down. But why was he wearing that mask?"

"Just in case we opened the door and saw him, I guess," Marco replied.

"Man, you told me last night that no human fist could hit the door that hard," Eugene Gerard reminded him. "What did you mean?"

"I don't believe he was using his fist, after the first few knocks," Marco answered. "I believe he was standing on the steps, jabbing that long pole against the door."

"Now about that loot," Lily said. "Since Jim Danton must have found where it was hidden, why didn't he put it in the bank?"

"Maybe he figured it had been in a safe place for nearly a hundred and fifty years, so why mess with it."

"And maybe he didn't trust banks any more than Hard Money Johnny did," Eugene Gerard suggested. "But you know, there's something that's been bothering me. Why didn't Hard Money Johnny tell his family where he'd hidden the stuff?"

Marco stretched the rubber mask out and let it snap back.

"I believe he told his son Willard," he replied, "and I guess Willard told his wife. But then they both died after Willard Danton's duel with Roy Knee, and the secret was lost."

"*Merr-ow!*"

Curious Cat was jabbing at the mask with both paws. Even when he played, he was dead serious.

"I wonder," the boy remarked, "are cats right or left handed?"

"Right or left pawed," Lily corrected. "The way he's going at it, Curious Cat looks like he's both."

Tires crunched on the driveway out front, and Sheriff Gross called, "Hey there, pard!"

Marco went out to the patrol car, followed by Lily and Eugene Gerard. Curious Cat was busy with the mask.

"I'm going back to try to talk some sense into Henri," the lawman told them. "Y'all want to come?"

"Can we, please?" Lily begged her great aunt, who had come to the front door.

"All right," she consented. "But don't fiddle with anything in the sheriff's car, and be back for lunch," she called as the three piled into the automobile.

On the ride, Lily, Eugene Gerard, and Marco took turns

telling the lawman about last night's adventure.

The bridge tender, white rooster in place, came out on his porch when the patrol car pulled up.

"Y'all come to arrest me?" he asked, laughing. Obviously, he was in a better mood than yesterday.

"No, Henri, we just wanted to know if you'd changed your mind about giving us those handwriting samples," the sheriff replied.

The bridge tender's good mood was going fast. "I don't change the mind, no."

"Wait a minute, Sheriff," Marco urged. "I just had an idea." He climbed out of the patrol car and walked up to the porch. "Mr. Cassatt," he asked softly, "is the reason why you won't give us a sample of your handwriting because you don't write?"

"I don't write, not too well, no," he told the rooster. "I sign the name on the salary check and that's all, yeah. I'm the fool, I reckon."

"No, sir, I don't believe so at all," the boy replied, "but thanks a lot."

"Funny, I reckoned everyone could read and write in this day and age," Sheriff Gross remarked after the boy told him his discovery. "Well, pard, you live and learn."

Live and learn, Marco thought. What was it Lily had said about Curious Cat? Something about his paws. . . . The boy asked her to repeat it.

She threw her hair over her face. "I don't remember," she said.

When they pulled up at Shady Hall, another automobile was parked in the driveway. They all piled out of the patrol car and trooped into the kitchen.

"Hi, kids," Dr. Slade greeted them from the kitchen table. "Just dropped by to see how y'all were making out. Hi, sheriff.

Still collecting handwriting samples?"

"We're about done with that, I expect," the lawman replied. "Maybe not, though."

"Dr. Slade was just about to write me a prescription for something to help me sleep nights," Miss Hazel explained. "That strawberry syrup stuff, as I told him, didn't work worth a hoot."

The doctor reached out his big right hand, picked up his gold pen from the table, and wrote rapidly on a small white pad, commenting, "This will do the trick."

"*Rrrr!*"

Curious Cat stalked into the kitchen, the Halloween mask hanging from his jaws like an enormous black and white rat. His front feet pushed out left, right, left under the flapping apron of the mask. What Lily had said about the animal's paws came back to Marco then.

"That's a nice pen, Doctor," he declared, picking it up. "Can I see it?"

Dr. Slade jumped to his feet. "If you don't mind, young man, that's my most valuable possession. May I have it back, please?"

"Catch!"

Marco tossed it about a foot over the doctor's head. Dr. Slade reached up his left hand and snatched the pen out of the air. His fingers closed on his most valuable possession, and the clapping noise was loud in the room. Slowly, Dr. Slade lowered his left hand. The eyes of everyone in the room—including the big, golden eyes of Curious Cat, Marco noticed—were on him.

"You use both hands," the boy said. "You're . . . I can't think of the word."

"Ambidextrous, pard," Sheriff Gross told him quietly.

"Ambidextrous," Marco repeated. "You wrote those letters to Miss Hazel with your left hand."

Curious Cat stalked into the kitchen, the Halloween mask hanging from his jaws like an enormous black and white rat....What Lily had said about his paws came back to Marco.

Dr. Slade sat back down at the kitchen table. Not a big man anyway, he seemed to have become smaller. A sigh filled the room, and the doctor seemed to become smaller yet.

"I've been checking on your house calls," the sheriff told him, "and I reckon you had enough time to make them and still drop by Shady Hall ever so often during the night. Dr. Slade, would you have any objection to giving me a specimen of your handwriting—with your *left* hand?"

The doctor glanced from the sheriff to Marco, then back to the sheriff. And then, with a tired shrug, he took the gold pen in his left hand and wrote on the prescription pad: "Get out of that house" and "That house is cursed."

"They're the same as the letters," Marco said.

"Dr. Slade, why don't we mosey on down to headquarters," the sheriff suggested. "Thanks, pard," he told Marco as he led the doctor out to the patrol car. "I'll be back to take you to the train."

After lunch, the boy put on his best clothes, then packed his bag to be ready to catch the 4:53 for New Orleans. And then he went into the study, with Miss Hazel, her grandniece, Eugene Gerard, and Curious Cat, listening as the grandfather clock ticked away the short while that remained for him at Shady Hall.

"Marco," Lily asked, "who's the guy that mailed all the letters?"

"I don't know," the boy replied, looking at the old leather book that Curious Cat had knocked off the shelf the other day. "The sheriff will have to find that out."

"From what you've said, man," Eugene Gerard told him, "I'm sorry good old Tad Payne wasn't in on this. I guess he's just a natural rotten-type fella."

"Every small town," Miss Danton told them grimly, "has its Tad Payne."

"I'm surprised Dr. Slade's the bad guy," Lily said. "He seemed like such a *good* guy."

Marco turned the yellowed pages of the leather book.

"I guess maybe he's like the *loup-garou* he told me about the first time I met him," the boy replied. "Only, instead of a full moon making him act crazy, it was money."

"Speaking of money," Eugene Gerard said, rubbing his hands together, "let's go find that two hundred thousand smackers!"

"Yeah," Marco agreed, "but where do we look? There's been a mess of people that have searched Shady Hall for it, including good old Dr. Slade.

"Miss Hazel," he asked, reading the faded brown handwriting on the first page of the leather book, "who's Catherine MacDuff Danton?"

"My great grandmother," Miss Hazel answered. "Is that her diary you have there? I haven't looked at that for years. She and my great grandfather, Edmund Danton, inherited Shady Hall after Jeremy Danton was killed when his horse threw him."

"Listen," Marco told them and read aloud:

" 'September Fifth, 1860. Arrived late today from New Orleans. A hot and dusty trip. But our first view of Shady Hall made it all worth while. It's easy to see how the tale started about the pot of gold being hidden here. Shady Hall is a most impressive . . . blah, blah, blah; blah, blah, blah.

"Listen: 'Edmund and I have a lovely bedroom on the southern side, overlooking Bayou Terrebonne—or "Bayou Terror," as the natives insist upon calling it . . . blah, blah, blah; blah, blah, blah.

" 'November Twenty-fifth: A raw, foggy day. We returned at sundown from a walk along Bayou T., and Edmund read the opening chapters of "Ivanhoe" in front of the fire in our room. . . .' "

"Marco," Lily told him, "if you say 'Blah, blah, blah' again, I'll hit you."

The boy turned the page, and found a green slip of paper —a New Orleans streetcar transfer.

" 'It was very pleasant,' he went on, " 'except that fireplace doesn't seem to have been built very well, and gives off more smoke than heat . . .' "

Marco gazed at the others:

"Y'all know what that means? The fireplace wasn't working right even *before* the Yankee shell hit the chimney!"

Lily tossed her hair back. "So what?"

"So I want to have a look at that fireplace," he replied. "And you know something else? Jim Danton must have read this part of the diary, too, because there's a New Orleans streetcar transfer on this page for a bookmark."

Miss Hazel found a big ring of rusty keys in a drawer of the kitchen cabinet. Her cheeks had color and her voice was tight as she told the boy, "The key to that room must be on here somewhere."

With Curious Cat in the lead, Marco next, followed by Lily, Eugene Gerard, and Miss Hazel, they climbed the stairs to the second floor and walked down the stained hallway to the door that badly needed paint. Curious Cat reached up, stretching, his claws scratching on the wood.

"He was trying to get us in here a long time ago," Lily said.

The fluttering sound and the musty smell came through the keyhole as Marco tried a dozen or more keys, without success. Downstairs, the grandfather clock announced it was four o'clock.

The next key slid into the lock and turned easily. With a squeal of rusty hinges, the door swung open. Miss Hazel and Lily screamed. A crowd of bats filled the room, swirling and squeaking. The four people waved their arms wildly to keep the little animals away. Then, in twos and threes, the bats fled through the broken pane of a window.

Marco went over to the iron fireplace, crouched down, and peered up the flue with his flashlight. Over his shoulder he said, "Something's blocking it."

He reached way up and took hold of the thing and tugged. Nothing happened, except that some soot fell. He tugged again with all his might.

Down in a cloud of black soot came a shower of gold and silver coins that bounced off his arms and face, jingling on the hearth. Gleaming through the fallen soot, he noticed a nice number of "Smiling Liberty" fifty dollar gold pieces, in addition to many other gold and silver coins.

"*Gungah!*"

"Brother!"

"Oh, man!"

"*Whew!*" (That was Miss Hazel.)

Most of the coins looked as though they had just come out of the New Orleans mint—instead of a sooty chimney, from inside a pair of greasy leather breeches, as they actually had.

"You see?" Marco asked the others. "Hard Money Johnny tied up the legs of these pants and hung them in the chimney to hold all his dough. Miss Hazel, your brother found the pants and emptied one of the legs. All these coins here were in the other leg."

"Marco, you're wonderful!" Miss Hazel exclaimed. "Y'all deserve a share in this, you know," she told the others.

"I just want a souvenir," the boy replied. He reached into the soot and found a small, beat-up silver coin. "Okay?"

She nodded, smiling.

It would make a neat addition to the two shark's teeth, his own tooth, the Minié ball, and the other items in his personal treasure trove.

A horn sounded outside, and Sheriff Gross yelled, "Hey, pard!"

"Cousin Marco," Lily told him, "you wash that soot off that face and those hands before you get on that train!"

Marco rushed down to the bathroom and did the best he could, then picked up his bag.

"Good-by, Miss Hazel."

"Good-by, Marco, and thank you. Thank you so much!"

"Good-by, Lily."

"Good-by, Marco."

"Good-by, pal."

"Good-by, pal."

"Where's Curious Cat?" the boy asked.

"I declare I don't know," Miss Hazel answered. "He was here a minute ago."

"Hey, pard!"

Suitcase in hand, Marco hustled out the front door, hearing the grumpy grandfather clock strike the quarter-hour. At the patrol car, the boy turned to look back through the light and shadows at Shady Hall.

"Good-by, Shady Hall," Marco said softly.

A large black animal was stretched on the grass, taking the afternoon sun. Carefully, he turned over on his back, his big golden eyes regarding the boy solemnly from their upside-down position.

"Good-by, Curious Cat."

"Good-by!"